Poppy Mayberry, The Monday

NOVA KIDS BOOK 1

Jennie K. Brown

TANTRUM BOOKS

Month9Books

POPPY MAYBERRY, THE MONDAY by Jennie K. Brown
All rights reserved. Published in the United States of America by Month9Books, LLC.
No part of this book may be used or reproduced in any manner whatsoever without written permission of the publisher, except in the case of brief quotations embodied in critical articles and reviews.
ISBN EPub: 978-1-944816-71-1 Mobi: 978-1-944816-72-8
ISBN Paperback: 978-1-944816-70-4
ISBN Hardback: 978-1-942664-96-3

Published by Tantrum Books for Month9Books, Raleigh, NC 27609
Cover Designed by Beetiful Book Covers
Cover Copyright © 2016 Tantrum Books for Month9Books

For Bennett

What if I fall?
Oh, but my darling, what if you fly?

– Erin Hanson

Poppy Mayberry,

The Monday

NOVA KIDS BOOK 1

Chapter One

The first time I knew for sure I was a Monday, I was sitting in one of Mrs. Flannagan's boring English lessons last year in fourth grade. She wanted to know if anyone could tell her the difference between smiles and meteors (that's what it looked like when I glanced at the board).

Of course, there was no way I could have possibly known the answer because I hadn't been paying attention. Mark Masters had been picking at his nose for like the last ten minutes, and that always distracted me a little. Total gross fest. Mark's in my class again this year and I feel sorry for him. Not because he still picks his nose, which he does, but because he is a Saturday. And Saturdays don't have any special powers.

"Who can tell me?" Mrs. Flannagan asked for the third time now, pushing her bright purple glasses up her bulbous nose. Her face grew pinker by the second.

From the corner of my eye I watched Ellie Preston's perfect little manicured hand shoot up. She always has the right answers. That's because she's a Thursday. And Thursdays read minds. Once, I thought that I wanted to be one too, but decided it would get exhausting always being in other people's thoughts. Plus, I wouldn't want to share Thursday with Ellie. I'd rather be forced to spend my evenings at Power Academy, or eat fried cockroaches with anchovy sauce. Yuck. Heck, I'd rather be a Saturday.

"Miss Preston," Mrs. Flannagan called, beaming.

Ugh.

Ellie perked up while pushing away from her face a few strands of long straight chestnut hair that had escaped from her obnoxious headband. She answered confidently as usual. "Similes compare two objects using the words 'like' or 'as.' Metaphors don't."

Ellie had the brightest, whitest smile that was always plastered across her face when answering a question. She pursed her lips and shot me an *of course YOU didn't know the answer, Poppy* kind of look. She's never liked me.

Cheater. You're not supposed to use powers in school, but Ellie got away with it, and still gets away with it today.

"You took the answer right out of my head, Ellie."

Mrs. Flannagan chuckled and her double chin jiggled right along like Jell-O. Cherry Jell-O. Her face always turned bright red when she taught about special literature terms. My best friend Veronica looked over at me and we rolled our eyes together.

Mrs. Flannagan kept babbling on and on about more English stuff. I zoned out again.

Ellie's desk sat right across from mine, so I could see her blue eyes darting around the room from person to person. I knew what she was doing—listening to thoughts. How could Mrs. Flannagan just ignore this? I couldn't wait for the day she would actually get punished. Ha. Ellie Preston sitting in Principal Wobble-Wible's office? That would be pretty much the most amazing thing ever.

I laughed to myself and imagined Ellie's fluorescent-pink-and-green headband flying off her perfect little head and breaking into teeny tiny pieces on the tiled floor below.

That's when it got weird. What I imagined actually happened.

In like a millisecond after my thought, the sparkly headband literally flew off her head, without a push, shake, or anything. It smashed on the SMART Board directly behind Mrs. Flannagan. The pieces scattered across the floor. A few of them even hit grossy Mark. His dirty finger immediately pulled out of his nose.

"Who did that?" Ellie's head whipped around and her

hair smacked Veronica in the face. Ellie's eyes searched down the rows, one by one. She was using her powers on us yet again. But at that point, who was I to comment on using powers? I put her in this position in the first place by using mine. I thought so, at least.

Before she got into my head, I quickly changed to thoughts of my dog Pickle. If Ellie looked in, she would see dog poop and dirty fur. Nothing that could incriminate me for what just happened.

But someone knew it was me. Veronica smirked. I winked back.

"Poppy Mayberry!" Mrs. Flannagan's nostrils flared as she stomped toward me like a big, red bull charging. "How dare you use your powers in this classroom!" Her pudgy hand pointed about a foot above the door to a plaque stating the number-one rule of Nova Elementary: NO POWER USAGE!

Although I should have been ashamed of the awful trick I had just played, I couldn't stop the giant smile from spreading across my face. Finally! My telekinesis was here. That's when I knew that I, Poppy Rose Mayberry, was officially a Monday.

Chapter Two

Pickle's wet tongue licked my face—my wakeup call just about every morning. I thought about forcing her to jump off the bed using my mind, but decided not to. Her five-pound furry self was just too darn cute. Plus, it could have ended badly.

"I know what you want," I said, scratching her in her favorite place—right behind her ears.

Pickle rolled over onto her back and begged me to rub her belly. So I reached my hand under her turquoise-and-purple trimmed doggy pajamas and did just what she wanted. Her little beady eyes looked toward her brush in the puffy purple dog bed next to my dresser. A high-pitched whimper escaped from her lips. Such a princess.

I could have easily jumped off my bed, taken two steps,

and grabbed the brush. What was the point of being a Monday if I didn't use my gift? I concentrated hard and imagined the brush lifting out of the plush bed and landing in my hand.

But it didn't. Instead, at what seemed like 200 miles-per-hour, it flew over my full-sized bed, bounced into the bright yellow wall, and crashed into the silver jewelry tree in the opposite corner of the room. Pickle yipped and her nails that desperately needed trimming *ticked* on the wood floor as she ran out of the room. Fail.

The plastic brush bristles were all tangled up in my dangling necklace tree. The beads clinked and clanged together, sounding like the wind chimes on the back porch. I never liked those wind chimes.

"Good morning, Poppy." Mom plopped down on my purple-striped down comforter and kissed the top of my head. Her red poufy hair bounced with the bed. Pickle hesitantly entered the room again.

"Were you just practicing?" She looked at me with … concern? Sadness? I wasn't sure. Both she and Dad had been waiting for me to gain total control over my Monday power, but it just hadn't happened yet, which was a total bummer. I frowned, taking in the scene around me.

"So you were practicing?" Mom's own necklaces and silver bracelets clinked and clanged together as she attempted to untangle Pickle's brush from the web of cord and beads.

"Seriously, Mom." I rolled my eyes. "I think you know the answer to that," I said, grabbing an orange pendant necklace from her hand and securing it around my neck. Just like pretty girl Ellie Preston, my mom was born on a Thursday in Nova, so she can read minds too. Of course, it's not always super fun having a mom who reads your thoughts.

"Honey, you will master those powers soon enough," Mom said for like the millionth time this week, reading me yet again. Or maybe the frown on my freckled face was a dead giveaway. Gosh, I hoped she was right. It had been a year since that first Monday power experience, and although I had made a little bit of progress with it, I was far from totally Monday-ing it up.

When that whole thing (and awesome thing I might add) happened with prissy Ellie's headband, I had thought it would be much easier to adjust to being a Monday. I assumed that it would come as easily to me as it did for everyone else at Nova. As the rest of the year went on, I watched everyone in my class quickly move along with their powers—everyone except me.

Luke Bender, he's a Wednesday, used his electricity manipulation power to turn off the lights on the last day of school—only four days after first discovering it. Sarah Simmion, a disappearing Friday, got so mad with Mrs.

Flannagan one day that she vanished from class and then invisibly walked back home—three weeks after her first disappearing episode. Right in the middle of class! She was promptly called to Principal Wobble-Wible's office the next morning. Even Mitchell Weiss, the teleporting Tuesday who had to repeat the fifth grade three times, mastered his power over the summer—only two months—I rest my case.

As for my Monday power, I soon learned that whole incident with Ellie's headband was just a fluke, and I was way behind everyone else. Bummer.

I thought back to the headband incident once again. "We are just so proud of our little Poppy Rose Mayberry, our precious Monday," my Dad had said that first day, ruffling my spirally orange hair that I had so carefully pulled back in a ponytail. Do you know how difficult it is to get every single crazy curly piece of out-of-control hair secured back in a band? Being a guy, my dad obviously didn't. I had told him and Mom about the headband incident over dinner that first night. Of course, Mom already knew about it.

"Well, how about a little demonstration then," she had said, pushing the serving bowl of spaghetti my way. "Now, just nice and slow, move the scoop, and dump some on my plate." Their expecting eyes had watched me closely, and they were beaming—obviously proud of their Monday of a daughter.

I remembered concentrating really, really hard ᵕ getting the spaghetti on the plate. How hard could it have been? Out of nowhere, the scoop had just catapulted marinara spaghetti across the dining room. Some gooey noodles stuck to the china cabinet behind my mom. Others hung from my Dad's bald head.

It was chaos. I could tell that they were trying to hold back frowns, and they gave one another a weird this-can't-really-be-our-daughter look. They knew what I knew—the whole power thing would not come easy to me.

I had looked across the table at my older brother Willie. He had a giant smirk on his face. He always found opportunities to rub in the fact that his teleporting Tuesday powers came in on the day he turned thirteen like clockwork. For some reason, Tuesdays get their powers later than other weekdays, but nevertheless, Willie's powers were right on time for a Tuesday. Unlike mine. Ugh.

"I guess we can't expect her to get them right away," Willie had said, throwing his napkin in my dad's face.

"Willie!" My mom looked toward my brother disapprovingly. But she was talking to an empty chair. He had disappeared on the spot, and was probably upstairs in his bedroom already.

"It takes time, Poppy." She had warmly smiled at me. But I could tell she was lying. Her power and Dad's Wednesday power came easy. They had told me years ago u get your power—you just get it. It clicks on

'itch. No Wednesday pun intended. I hated

_ . disappointment to them. I mean, it was almost a year since the headband and spaghetti incidents, and I couldn't even keep Pickle's brush from flying across my bedroom.

"Just practice a little more after school today. It will come soon enough, Poppy," Mom reassured me, bringing me back to the sad reality that was my powerless life. By the look on her face, I could tell that she was reassuring herself as well. I hoped she was right. It was embarrassing how far behind I was compared to other people in my class. And at this rate, there was a huge possibility that I might get sent to Power Academy—the last place I want to spend my weeks this summer—away from my friends, away from my family and away from Pickle. Hello! I do have plans. My best friend Veronica White (she's a Monday, too … but a much better Monday than me) and I wouldn't be able to hang out if I was forced to go to Power Academy for the totally power-challenged rejects.

I heard whining and saw Pickle's cute little face looking up at me. Even after the disastrous attempt a few minutes ago, she still wanted to be brushed. What a trooper. I sighed, and decided to do it the old-fashioned way—by hand. There was no way I would try to use my Monday power with the possibility of taking out one of her eyes.

Chapter Three

I got to school and let out a sigh of relief after noticing that Ellie's desk had been moved up toward the front of the room and far away from me. Ever since the headband incident last year, which was a total accident, she had been meaner to me than usual. For instance, two weeks ago, I tripped in the cafeteria and my whole tray of ravioli flew all over the floor and onto my brand new flats. Geesh, what's with me and spilling Italian food?

Ellie looked at me with those crazed-meanie eyes. "Aww ... not only is Poppy lagging behind in the power department, she can't even walk without being a total loser." Then she let out this horrible wicked-witch-like cackle. Seriously, I think she may have even had a green hue to her face. If Mrs. Flannagan hadn't been on cafeteria duty watching me with those equally evil eyes of hers, I would have grabbed a handful of ravioli messiness and thrown it on Ellie's white capris and pink purse.

Ellie's BFF Celia Green was staring in my direction, too. She had that same annoying smirk on her face that Ellie did. Celia's also a Monday, and I just knew Ellie told her to make me trip somehow. Those girls are unbelievable!

Another time of utter meanness was just last week during gym class. Ellie asked if I would be her partner in tennis. Not to brag, but I am pretty good at that game. Both my parents played in college. The whole hand-eye coordination just comes kind of naturally to me. Too bad my powers weren't coming in the same way.

I knew Ellie would act even worse if I didn't say yes, so I decided to be the bigger person and agreed to partner up with her. Well, that was a huge mistake.

"Now take it easy, Poppy. You know I'm no good at this game," Ellie had warned just as I was about to serve. I threw the tennis ball up and gently lobbed it over the net. Seriously, I could not have hit it any softer.

In one swift movement Ellie tennis-shuffled to her left and whacked the ball so hard I could practically feel the air coming from the racket. The strings made direct contact with the ball, and it flew toward me so fast that I couldn't get my racket up in time to stop it from bouncing off my head. I immediately fell to the ground. I felt the goose-egg bump forming right away. It took two days for the swelling to go down. Once again, I heard Ellie's obnoxious laugh coming from the other side of the net as Veronica ran to my rescue.

Ellie was totally faking me out. With that perfect shuffle and a hit that fast, she absolutely knew how to play tennis. And then the words came from her pretty, pink lip-glossed mouth. "If you were a real Monday, you would've been able to stop it." Ugh! What a witch!

Anyway, those were just two specifics of the many examples of her utter cruelty. It was hard to believe that we grew up just doors away, and a few years ago we were playing with dolls in her enormous, perfectly pink, perfectly decorated toy room. A lot can change in a few short years, even though I wasn't sure why things changed in the first place. Out of nowhere, she started treating me like we were the world's biggest enemies. Last year's headband incident multiplied that by ten.

And now, I watched as Ellie twirled her perfectly sculpted hair around her perfectly manicured fingers. She wasn't even paying attention to Mr. Salmon's lesson on Roman numerals. Well, none of us really were. I mean Mark's finger was lost in his nose. Just like my powers, some things never change. I chuckled to myself.

"*Psst*," I heard behind me. I turned around to see Veronica shaking her head. She quickly scanned the room then tossed a piece of paper my way. It landed a few feet from my desk. I glanced up to make sure Mr. Salmon was still in his own Roman-numeral world, and carefully reached down and over to grab it.

Sort of intercepted this was written on the front flap in Veronica's handwriting.

I looked back again at my best friend. Her head was still shaking, and her blue eyes looked almost sad. *Open it,* she mouthed to me with urgency as her eyes darted back up toward Mr. Salmon.

I unfolded the paper in front of me. At first glance, I noticed it was a note that had been passed back and forth between two students. It was obvious to me because that's how Veronica and I communicate during class. She always writes in a blue pen and mine is always purple. But the two pen colors in this note were pink and orange. It totally didn't have our blue and purple hallmark.

I glanced over toward Ellie and watched her pink pen tap the desk. Her partner-in-crime and BFF Celia was twirling an orange one between her fingers. I put two and two together, and then began to read.

Pink: Can u even believe she is wearing that! Lol

Orange: 4 real. Who even tries to pull off velvet headbands anyway?

I reached up to the top of my head and sighed once I felt the soft purple headband that my mom bought me for Christmas last year. Don't they have anything better to write about?

Pink: And what about those necklaces? She wears that orange one like every day.

Orange: Lol. To match her crazy hair! See what she is thinking about …

Pink: She is nervous about Power Academy for the power rejects. Of course she's going. I heard she can't even make a pencil move without stabbing someone.

Orange: That is ridiculous!

Pink: What a loser.

I made sure neither of the mean girls were looking my direction before I crumpled up the note and pushed it under my notebook. I felt a few tears begin to form in the corner of my eyes. Seriously, didn't these girls have anything better to talk about than me? They were first-class bullies.

And what they said about Power Academy was just wrong. Sure, I'm not as good at the whole telekinesis thing as the other Mondays in my class, but that didn't mean I would have to spend day after day of misery there—with the other … well … powerless rejects.

"Miss Mayberry? What seems to be the problem?" Mr. Salmon asked, jolting me from my thoughts. His toupee looked like a giant fur-ball bouncing on his head as he walked toward me. It would usually make me laugh, but I was definitely not laughing at this moment.

I quickly wiped the wetness from my cheeks and shoved the corner of the note farther under my notebook. At this point all eyes were on me- including Ellie's. Her lips curved into an I-hate-you smile.

"I … um …"

"You know that I don't appreciate people passing notes in my class. Especially during my math lessons," he smile-yelled and his big eyes bulged out of their sockets. You just don't mess with his math lessons.

"I wasn't …" I tried to protest.

His skinny fingers reached down and pushed my notebook to the side. He grabbed the folded up piece of paper and took it to the front of the room. Everyone remained silent. *Please don't read it out loud*, I thought to myself.

Leaning against his desk, Mr. Salmon folded the note back up, shook his head, scanned the room (I assumed looking for the owner of the pink and orange pens), and spoke. "I should have done this quite some time ago. To Mr. Wible's office, both of you." Mr. Salmon pointed directly at me and then at Ellie. Everyone else in the class made the typical, "ahhhhh" sound when anyone gets sent to the principal's office.

"You should know that I, of all people Mr. Salmon, would never mean to intentionally interrupt your amazing lessons," Ellie snipped. I'm pretty sure 90 percent of the class rolled their eyes. She sure was full of it.

"I don't want to hear it, Miss Preston. Off to the office for you." He looked at me. "And Miss Mayberry, let's get moving along."

I grabbed my bag, caught a sympathetic glance from Veronica, and walked out the door, wishing that I were a Friday and could have just disappeared right then and there.

Chapter Four

In the five years that I had been a student at Nova Elementary, I had never been sent into the principal's office. Not until Mr. Salmon sent me.

Ellie Preston sat across from me on a wooden bench completely avoiding eye contact. We were waiting outside the main office for our turn with Nova Elementary's "esteemed principal." (That's what was written on his door. Ugh.) Esteemed? Yeah, right!

"You, like, totally know this is all your fault," Ellie's voice screeched. She rolled her eyes and pulled a nail file from her purse. Diva. Who even carries a nail file to school?

I didn't give her the satisfaction of a response. I couldn't even imagine how she thought this was even remotely my fault. She continued filing, and I cringed at every sawing motion. That awful grinding sound always gets on my nerves. She leaned toward me, reached her hand out so that it was practically in my face, and continued just sawing away. Stupid mind-reading Thursday.

"Ugh." I sighed.

"Ugh." Ellie sighed, and then she used the file to point toward the principal's door. "And you know that we are totally going to get at least like five days of detention from Mr. Wobble-Wible in there," she said, rolling her eyes again, and then continued, "and unlike you, *I* have things to do this summer."

I brushed off her last comment, and as much as I tried not to smirk, I did. I thought that Veronica and I were the only two that had a nickname for Principal Wible. Wobble-Wible. I know it sounded kind of mean saying that, but Mr. Wible kind of wobbles when he walks. Really, it's more like a waddle. But whatever you want to call it. With a shiny bald head and wobbly gait, he simply looks like a penguin in a suit.

The door creaked open, and Noah Summers, a Sunday with no powers, but kinda cute anyway, shuffled out with his head hanging down to his chest. Must not have gone well with Wobble-Wible for him.

"Miss Preston and Miss Mayberry, you're up next," Wobble-Wible shouted and Ellie tossed the nail file back into her over-sized pink (of course) purse.

We quietly entered his office and sat down on the other side of the desk in two tan and red checkered chairs that were so humongous they practically swallowed us whole. Before I could even look up at his face, my eyes stopped on the paperweight holding down a stack of files. I laughed a little inside. What were the chances? A penguin.

I'm pretty sure Ellie saw it too or read it in my mind because when she caught my eye for a split second it was like we shared some inside joke. Her head snapped back to attention as Wobble-Wible cleared his throat and began.

"Ladies, I don't know what exactly is going on between the two of you." Wobble-Wible's also one of those people who overemphasizes his "Ts." "But it has been brought to my attention that there have been a few incidents over the past—"

"I have never done anything to *her*," Ellie cut him off, protesting while sitting up and crossing her arms over her pink T-shirt. Her head snapped toward me and she smiled, batting her long eyelashes. "Right, Poppy?"

Mr. Wible and I rolled our eyes in unison. Maybe he was on my side after all.

"I don't want to hear any disputes, just listen to what I have to say, Miss Preston." Wobble-Wible's voice was firmer with Ellie than I imagined it would ever be considering the fact that she was the "perfect" Nova student.

"Not only has there been some incidents involving you

and Poppy, but I have also been *told* that you, Miss Preston, have been illegally using your powers in school."

Yes! Finally, someone noticed. Who better than the head principal?

He picked up the penguin. I laughed inside again, and then watched as he pulled a manila folder from underneath of it. From the corner of my eye, I noticed that Ellie shifted a little in her seat. Her ballet flats nervously clicked on the floor below. He opened the file.

"It seems that you have not only been using your powers to read the thoughts of other students, but you have also been taking advantage of some teachers as well." His eyes searched Ellie's for a response. "Isn't that right, Miss Preston?" he prompted.

"Well ... I ..." she stuttered. And then defensively added, "Only when I absolutely ne—"

"You know the number one rule here, and so you must feel the repercussions of your prohibited actions." Wobble-Wible's also one of those people who likes to use big words—like prohibited, epitome, and metaphor.

At this point in the conversation, it seemed as if I were a non-factor in this whole situation. If I just slipped out the door, Wobble-Wible may not have even noticed.

"Because you have been so negligent with your Thursday powers, I find that we must do something about reining them in, and keeping them under control." His stubby fingers reached behind him and grabbed a large binder. I couldn't quite make out what was written on the front. "You need to learn the proper *t*ime and place for weekday power usage. Since you so recklessly use them in school where they are no*t* allowed, who's *t*o s*t*op you from using them ou*t*side of the Nova ci*t*y limi*t*s?" Wobble-Wible continued. "Could you even imagine wha*t* *outsiders* would *t*hink? *T*hey would—" He stopped there.

Ellie slouched in the chair, and stared at the clock above his head. "I guess I can try to do a better job with them," she said unconvincingly while twirling a few strands of brown hair around her finger.

Mr. Wible laughed. "You're going *t*o have *t*o do a li*tt*le more than *t*ry, Ellie. And I'm going *t*o see tha*t* you do so."

He slid the binder across the large desk, and I could now make out the cover. An audible laugh escaped from my lips.

Ellie rolled her eyes, yet again, and sat back up to reach for the binder. "Ohhhh, no, no, no, no, no." She stood up with hands firmly planted on her hips. "There's nooo way I am going there." Her filed finger wiggled at Mr. Wible and then she leaned down and rummaged through her purse. I assumed she was looking for the new rhinestone cell phone she showed off to our entire class last week.

"No use calling them, Ellie. Your paren*t*s are in comple*t*e agreement," he said, totally using his own Thursday mind-reading powers on her. "You're already enrolled in the Academy."

Her breath came out in quick, short bursts. "I can't leave my friends behind. There is no way I am going to that place …" she stuttered, "… alone."

"Oh, you won't be attending Power Academy alone," Mr. Wible reassured her. That's when his beady eyes meet mine. I panicked, sure of the words that were about to fly from his mouth. Knowing that I, too, needed a whole lot of work in the whole Monday power department.

"Poppy Mayberry will be joining you."

Ugh. These were going to be the longest months of my life.

Chapter Five

"So, you're telling me that you have to spend, like, the entire summer at Power Academy?" Veronica blinked hard. "With Ellie?"

I threw the Power Academy brochure down on the table in front of her. The bright reds and blues on the pamphlet made the place actually look appealing, but I knew that wasn't the case.

My shoulders dropped. This day couldn't possibly get any worse. "Yep." I finally answered. I'd been trying to deny that little fact for the last two hours—ever since Wobble-Wible told me the worst news I'd ever heard in my entire life. I mean, who in their right mind wants to be stuck in the prison that is Power Academy? Not to mention the fact that everyone knows that it is a last resort for the powerless and power delinquents. You might as well be a Saturday or Sunday with no powers whatsoever! Sometimes I thought about how easy my life would be if that were the case.

When I told Veronica about this horrible news, she suggested we go to Novalicious—the BEST ice-cream-dessert café in the world to cheer me up a bit. How could I say no? They have over one hundred different ice cream flavors.

"Well, thank goodness I got my powers nice and early," she unknowingly bragged while taking a lick from her cone. "And extra thank goodness that I don't have to go to that awful place. Blech!" Veronica looked disgusted. "I'd rather be forced to eat a sauerkraut-stuffed piece of duck liver than go there."

I love my best friend, but she has no filter whatsoever and absolutely no concept of when she makes offensive comments. Was it necessary to rub it in that much?

"Thanks a lot," I said, looking down at the delicious double-scoop chocolate peanut butter ice cream cone in my hand that, for some reason, now seemed a bit unappetizing after Veronica's duck liver comment. "Way to make me feel better about the situation." I threw my cone toward the trashcan to my left. But just as quickly as it went toward the metal can, it flew back in my direction. I snatched it with my hand in mid-air. Cone first. I didn't want to risk a chocolatey, sticky mess on my favorite purple tunic.

Veronica smirked. "You would totally regret throwing that away," she said with a wink.

I laughed along with her, even if her Monday gesture was just another reminder of my own total lack of skills. I glanced around Novalicious to see all sorts of other people using their weekday powers. Mrs. Evans, my first grade teacher and another Monday, was using her telekinesis to move a napkin up and down her toddler's cheek. After paying at the counter, Mr. Ellison and his oldest son Trevor (both Tuesdays) disappeared. I assumed that they teleported back home. Even though I knew that they weren't all intentionally showing off, I just felt like they were purposely emphasizing that they were awesome at their powers when I was significantly less than awesome.

"Look, Poppy. You are totally going to be fantabulous," Veronica stated in between bites of her gummy-bear covered vanilla ice cream. A white dribble ran down her chin. It seemed everyone had confidence in me besides … well … me.

And to be honest, being away from home scared me. I could only name on one hand the few things that I was afraid of. Truly afraid of. I'm not talking about my two totally irrational fears of turkey stuffing and Mr. Salmon's toupee that looks like a furry, gray animal sitting on the top of his head. I'm talking about true fears. And Power Academy was one of mine. I'd heard that it was a mix of intense school classes and boot camp. Although I'm pretty good at school, I didn't want to make a fool of myself in the power boot-camp classes. Not to mention the crazy Headmistress Larriby. I'd heard nothing but bad and scary stories about that woman.

Not only that, but I had never been away from Mom and Dad for more than a weekend—and that weekend once a year was usually spent on vacation with Veronica. So at least then I had someone awesome to be with. But this summer, I would be away from them all.

"We'll write to each other like every week," Veronica said, snapping me from my self-wallowing. "I just don't understand how they expect you to stay there if they don't even give you the courtesy of using a phone." She Monday-powered her napkin into the trashcan. "I mean, welcome to the twenty-first century, Power Academy People!"

Although it was going to stink being away from Mom, Dad, and Veronica, I was comforted by one thing—Pickle got to come with me. Other than the basic necessities of clothes and stuff, each student *invited* (yes, they actually call it *invited* even though I am pretty sure we're all *forced* to go which is pretty ridiculous) to Power Academy could bring one favorite personal item from home.

The examples for personal items stated in the brochure were things like instruments, board games, sports equipment, and stuff like that. The items listed in the prohibited items section were things like cell phones, Xboxes, iPods, and electronic stuff that Wednesdays could totally tamper with if they were not so hot with their powers. And considering where these Wednesdays had to spend their summer, there was no way they were good.

"Here's a thought," Veronica said, her pitch slightly raised. "Why don't I come along as your personal item?"

I couldn't tell if she was serious or not, and pointed to a sentence written in bold on page twelve, *Other individuals do not constitute as personal items.*

"Oh." She frowned. "It was a shot!"

But, the one thing the brochure didn't say anything at all about was animals. So my favorite thing that would be staying with me at Power Academy really wasn't a thing at all. Heck, she was practically one of the family. My cute dog Pickle would definitely help me get through those next few months.

The next morning, I started packing up my summer clothes and Pickle's. Yes, my Yorkie wears clothing.

"Only three months," I reassured Mom a week later as she drove me to Nova Elementary where the bus would pick me—us (Pickle)—up and then drop us off at Power Academy thirty minutes later. She was not taking my departure well at all.

"Poppy, it's just that—" Her watery eyes looked away.

"Only three months," I said again, touching her shoulder and calming her down before she started crying again like she did this morning. And that one this morning was a gusher. My shirt was soaked. If she cried like that again, then I'd cry. Crying was, like, contagious to me.

"Just … don't be afraid of your powers," she said, locking eyes with mine.

What? What an odd choice of words. *Powers?* All her crying and crazy emotions must have gotten the best of her. Why the heck would I be afraid of being a Monday?

She turned her body toward me and her bracelets clanged together as she enveloped me in a hug. The seatbelt made me choke a little bit. "Okay, Mom." I pulled away. "Love you." Her blue eyes squinted as her lips curled up into that proud-mother kind of a smile.

"Love you too, Poppy."

When we got out of the car she hugged me insanely tight one last time, and I inhaled her floral perfume, hoping to take some of her with me.

Chapter Six

"Hey, there. Can you scoot over?" A boy's voice said while I was getting situated in the too-small bus seat. I guess they wanted to make everything about this summer miserable—starting with the bus. But really? Would it hurt them to make the seats just a little bit bigger?

"I really don't understand why I have to go to this stupid place," the boy next to me continued while angrily shoving his duffle bag in the overhead compartment. I looked up to see that he was about my age. A few pieces of sandy blond hair fell into his green eyes. He flicked them away with the back of his hand. If I were a better Monday, I could have easily moved them out of his face for him. But I'm not, and that's why I was on my way to Power Academy.

"I was supposed to go on vacation with my friend and

his family, but those plans were ruined," he continued and leaned back in the seat. He huffed loudly.

I smiled and rolled my eyes. Totally got it. "I know the feeling," I said under my breath, glancing down at Pickle in her purple travel carrier. Her cute little sleepy face looked up at me.

"I'm Logan Elliot Prince." His hand shot out at me, taking me off guard. No one my age usually shakes hands.

But I shook it back. "Poppy Rose Mayberry," I said, since he was into using full names. I tried to figure out what day he was, but couldn't. "What are—"

"Friday. A Friday that *they* say needs some help." He sighed, and I followed his cold gaze and head nod to a cute old couple standing next to the bus. They must have been his grandparents.

"They don't look so bad." I said, noticing the sad looks on their wrinkly faces. "So, why exactly—"

"Oh, they say I'm just a little behind, that's all." He cut me off once again. "Like they would even know." His eyes rolled. If he hadn't just told me that he's a Friday, then I definitely would have thought that he was a Thursday. Especially with the way he seemed to be answering my questions before I could even get them out. Rude much?

"I haven't seen you—"

"That's cause I just—"

"Would you please stop doing that?" I asked, probably

a tad bit too forcefully while staring into those twinkling green eyes of his.

He folded his arms over his chest. "Whoooaaa. Soorrrry," he huffed loudly and turned his head toward the aisle. A few other students looked back.

Touchy, touchy. Ridiculous. Great—a fun bus ride with an emotional Friday who couldn't even disappear if I wanted him to.

I tapped his shoulder. "Okay. Since we are going to be sitting next to each other for, like, the next million minutes, you might as well just give up and talk to me now," I said.

Silence.

"So … I will try again."

His arms crossed over his chest again and he sighed. This might be harder than I thought.

"I haven't seen you around Nova Elementary. Did you just move here or something?" I asked in my nicest, sweetest voice, hoping this would prompt an answer. I even batted my eyelashes like I had seen Ellie do at Evan Finklestein when she needed to borrow a pencil. After I asked Logan the question, though, I realized that it didn't make much sense considering the fact that if you had weekday powers, you were 100% born in Nova. But maybe he had moved away and come back.

Silence.

He finally turned his head back toward me and stared.

And stared some more …

Silence.

"Awkward," I said to Pickle under my breath, fully aware that Logan heard. She yawned and put her furry head down to sleep more.

Finally, the stubborn boy gave in. "I just want to make sure you are finished with what you need to ask so I don't cut you off again," he said with a hint of sarcasm, but I noticed the crooked smile he stifled back.

"Haha, Mister SmartyPants." I chuckled.

"I've lived in Nova my whole life." He paused and looked toward the floor. He spoke quietly, "Well, Mom and Dad died a little while back."

I couldn't even imagine something bad happening to one parent, let alone both. Poor Logan. "How did they di—"

"My grandparents take care of me now." He cut me off. I wasn't sure if it was out of habit or if he was avoiding the question. I was probably too forward in asking anyway.

I shrugged and moved on. "So why haven't I seen you around school?"

"Well, my grandma thinks that I will get the best education at home," he said, imitating his grandmother's voice, and he did a pretty good job of making that scratchy old lady voice. "But I'm on this bus to Power Academy, so I guess that's not working too well."

We chuckled together.

"Plus, both of my grandparents are totally over-protective. I'm actually surprised they are sending me here—since that's where ..." He paused. "Never mind. I don't mind the whole home-schooling thing though," he continued, changing the touchy subject.

"Mmmhmm," I mumbled. I wondered what he was going to say, but decided not to press the issue. And that whole home-schooling thing I didn't get. Who in their right mind "wouldn't mind" being home-schooled? I would totally miss the whole socializing aspect—even if I only had one true friend.

"I told my grandparents that I refuse to spend my summer at the *prison* that is Power Academy, but they wouldn't listen," he said. "Pop's a Sunday, and Gram's a Saturday, so it's not like they would even understand any powers at all." Then he whispered, "And for the record ..." He looked around to make sure nobody noticed, and then winked at me. "I *do* know what I'm doing."

For some reason I felt a little nervous and looked down to see Pickle's belly move up and down with each sleepy breath. When I brought my head back up, Logan was nowhere to be found. When I looked down the rows I didn't see him anywhere there either. "Definitely a Friday," I muttered to a passed-out Pickle. Logan had disappeared. I guess he *did* know what he was doing after all. So why was he even on this bus?

My body jerked to the right as we turned at a road sign that read *No Trespassing*. Pickle jolted awake as we continued down a windy dirt path surrounded by a forest of dark green trees. There was the outline of a mansion-looking building on the horizon. If I squinted hard enough, I thought I noticed some other buildings deep in the forest. The forest that I heard was haunted. A slight shiver went down my spine. "Almost there," the bus driver yelled.

"And Logan is still missing," I said to Pickle, shrugging my shoulders. Even though it shouldn't have mattered if he was there or not, my cheeks grew warm at the thought that I could get along with this Logan Elliot Prince.

Chapter Seven

"Okay, kiddos. Single file, now. Single file into the main hall," a large woman in a way-too-tight green dress screamed as we got off the bus and made our way under the giant arches that read Power Academy, Home of the Specials. The second part of the sign made it really obvious that we were here because we weren't quite up to speed. The specials? Really? I rolled my eyes and thought that this would be something that Veronica and I would totally laugh about if she were here.

I instantly recognized this rotund woman from the brochure as Headmistress Larriby. Rumored to be the meanest and cruelest woman not only at Power Academy, but in the entire Nova township, this was one woman I hoped to never meet. Veronica told me that she heard from

Mark Masters who heard from his cousin that last summer at P.A. (Power Academy), Mrs. Larriby forced a boy to spend a week in the supposedly haunted forest surrounding campus just because he couldn't turn off a light with his Wednesday power. Ridiculous. I wondered what she would think about and do because of my lack of skills.

"I also heard that that boy disappeared and hasn't been found since," Veronica had added at the tail-end of the story. Sure, she always knew the good gossip, but sometimes she had a tendency to exaggerate things, so I could never be certain. "They were never sure if he was eaten by bears or swooped up by ghosts. But either way, he hasn't returned to this day," she had added with extreme hand gestures for extra effect.

We were greeted (if that's what you want to call it) by Headmistress Larriby and a skinny guy who had his back toward us. Bald patches of skin poked through thinning gray hair, and he obviously had a tough time choosing clothing, because his red sweatshirt swallowed him whole. When he finally turned around, I gasped back a chuckle. A thick forest of hairs stuck out both sides of his nose that I could see from like ten feet away. Gross. I think it was even worse than Mark Masters's nose-picking habit.

As each student walked under the arches, nostril-man handed us those squishy stress-ball things. The silver font on the front of them said *Embrace Your Day, Be Special.*

I guess they were our consolation prizes for being forced here this summer. He winked at me as he plopped it in my hand. What a weirdo.

"Here ya go, Pickle," I said tossing the ball, now her newest toy, into her travel den. She gave me an approving *yip* and her tail wagged back and forth in excitement. Love that little fur ball!

"Hey, check out the beak on that one," Logan said, pointing to nostril man. He reappeared next to me in line and rested his forearm on my head. Not the first time someone did that. Oh, the perks of being vertically challenged.

I nudged him. "Single file. You better watch out or Old Woman Larriby is gonna send you to the haunted forest and you'll disappear for a lot longer than that little bit on the bus." I looked around to make sure nobody was listening. "By the way …" I hesitated a second before continuing, "Where did you go earlier?"

Since my seat partner-in-crime disappeared within the first ten minutes of the trip here, and everyone else on the bus was engrossed in other conversations about their lacking skills, I was left to talk to myself and Pickle the rest of the way. Although Pickle was so cute and pretty decent company, the only conversation she can keep is one involving whining, whimpering, and a *yap* at the mention of the occasional treat.

"Just up and down the rows, listening in on conversations," Logan answered quietly as Mrs. Larriby passed by.

"Then you must be pretty good with your powers."

He smirked. "From what I overheard, I'm better than most on the bus."

Apparently, he was cocky, too, but I didn't mind.

"It comes and goeeeee ... ouch!"

Before he could even finish his sentence, Logan's head jerked backward as Headmistress Larriby grabbed a handful of his hair and pulled him behind me in line. Ouch.

"That looked painful."

"You're tellin' me," he said, rubbing the back of his head.

"Eyes up here, all." Mrs. Larriby waited for silence and then continued. "Our welcome session begins in the library at eighteen-hundred," she screamed even though we were all within like ten feet in front of her. "Be there early to ensure a seat," she added and spun around on her matching icky-green heels, and that was it.

In the very few lessons of Mr. Salmon's that I actually paid attention to, military time was one of them. Go figure.

Eighteen minus twelve. "Six o'clock," I whispered over my shoulder to Logan.

He laughed.

Headmistress Larriby and her huge-nostril sidekick

disappeared (not literally, like a Friday would) into the next room over. Everyone jumped out of line and chatter erupted.

I used this opportunity to take a good look around the place. There were probably about thirty other Weekday kids here. I recognized maybe half of them from Nova Elementary. A few others were going to be 7th graders who must have flunked out last summer (bummer), and I was assuming the rest were in the same home-schooling situation as Logan.

It seemed that many of them already knew each other or were making friends quickly. I couldn't complain. I was sure that I could potentially have a good friend in Logan.

Right away, I noticed the group of Thursdays huddled in the far corner. Their eyes darted around from person to person. I had seen Ellie and my mom do this enough to know that they were attempting to read minds. But by the anguished looks on their faces, and the fact that they were here, I had a feeling that those Thursdays weren't having much success.

Some other students chatted by the water fountain right outside the library. One of them pointed toward the giant chandelier hanging right in the center of the foyer. He was a Wednesday, I assumed, who was trying to make the lights cut out. No such luck.

Three Fridays were sitting on the edge of the master

staircase that sat between two long hallways. Again, I could tell by their strained squinty faces that they were trying really hard to disappear. I remembered back to 4th grade when Colby Mason first disappeared in the middle of Mr. Harbow's classroom. These Fridays had the same exact kind of constipated look on their faces that Colby had on his that day. I giggled as their lips and cheeks contorted and scrunched harder. I guess Logan really was ahead of the game.

Of course, there were no Tuesdays here, because all of Nova knows that Tuesdays don't get their power until they are thirteen years old. Sometimes I wished I were a Tuesday. I would teleport right out of this place faster than the speed of light and be back in my bedroom playing with Pickle and hanging out with my family.

Although the sign out front said that Power Academy was established in 2001, I found that hard to believe. Yes, the façade was beautiful, but from what I could see of the interior, it looked pretty dilapidated. On every wall in the entranceway, the floral wallpaper was peeling off to reveal a dark color underneath. The winding wooden staircase had more than a few missing rungs. The whole place truly looked like a house out of a scary movie. Not gonna lie, it kind of gave me the creeps, and that's hard to do. Maybe that's one of the ways they force us students into mastering our powers. I mean, who would want to come back here another summer? Then I noticed the boy standing directly to my left. He looked old enough to drive. Poor guy must have failed out of this place a bunch of times.

Pickle began to whine. She had been in her travel home for a while now. I grabbed her purple and orange-striped collar and leash, and let her walk around a little. "Hey there, little guy," Logan said as Pickle's little legs ran to him.

"Little girl," I corrected him and smiled.

He pushed a piece of hair from his face and then reached down, way down, to pet her. Her tailed wiggled back and forth so fast that I thought she might lift right off the ground. She rolled over on her back, begging him to pet her belly. Definitely spoiled.

"Pickle," I said, reaching down and petting her too. "Meet my new friend, Logan."

At the mention of the word *friend*, I noticed Logan smile, but I didn't bring that to his attention.

And then I heard it. Her. Ugh.

"Like, Oh. My. Gosh. I have been looking for you, like, all over, Poppy," a shrill, annoying voice came from behind me. I would know that voice anywhere.

"Hey, Ellie," I mumbled, unenthused as she stepped up next to me and gave me one of those fake "air-kisses" you see rich ladies do in the movies. I just stood there stiff as a board, not knowing how to react. She turned to the door and flicked her wrist at the uniformed man standing in the frame. On her command, the chauffeur exited. That explained why she hadn't been on the bus. Ugh.

"And whoooo's this, Poppy?" Ellie asked, looking Logan up and down, flicking her chestnut hair from her shoulder. She beamed, just like she did when she won Little Miss Nova, 2015.

"This is Logan. We met today on the—"

"Well, it is so awwwwesome to meet you, Loooh-gan." Ellie stuck out her French-tipped hand for him kiss (who does that, anyway?), and locked eyes with him. I'd seen that look enough times to know that she was trying to read his mind. He didn't know what to do with her hand, so he just dropped it. For some reason, I felt relieved.

"Oh," she said, confused, not used to rejection.

I laughed and looked up at the old grandfather clock in the corner of the foyer and saw that we had five minutes until Headmistress Larriby would come hunt us down.

"We should probably go in," I said to Logan. And only to Logan.

"Yes, we certainly must," Ellie squeaked, grabbing Logan's hand and dragging him into the library. Ugh.

By the time I got Pickle packed up in her bag, all the seats in the library had been taken. I looked around to see that the only chair available was the one on the platform where I'm sure Larriby would be sitting in a few minutes.

If my Monday powers worked like they were supposed

to, then I would have floated that chair right over to me in the back of the room and taken a seat before Headmistress Larriby even arrived. But they didn't work that way and so I was here. In Power Academy you-know-what.

Headmistress Larriby bounced into the room, because she really was quite bulbous, with Nostril-Man, which was all I knew to call him at this point. She took a quick glance around and then made direct eye contact with me. I could tell by the look on her face that she was not happy whatsoever. In fact, she looked downright angry.

"Did I not say to be in this room a few minutes before eighteen-hundred?" her voice echoed across the library and hit me so hard that I felt a little off-balance.

The large room suddenly felt tiny. In an instant, I sensed thirty sets of Weekday eyes on me. My pulse began to quicken, and I was positive that I had begun to turn red. If only Ellie hadn't distracted me and I had been in the room like two seconds earlier to grab a chair, I wouldn't have been in this awkward situation. Stupid Ellie.

Headmistress Larriby's arm fat jiggled while she waved them around, screaming at me using words like "tardy" and "unacceptable" and "disrespectful." All the other students were silent. I took a quick glance at Ellie to notice her lips curved into an evil little smile, of course. Logan looked like he wanted to save me and make *me* disappear. If only he could.

I squeezed Pickle a little bit tighter to my chest, closed my eyes, and took a deep breath, wishing I were back in my house in Nova. When I opened my eyes once again to see Headmistress Larriby still rattling on about my tardiness, I did something that surprised even me. I imagined that chair up on stage sliding swiftly away from Mrs. Larriby's grasp.

With her eyes still locked on mine, Old Jiggly Jell-O Arms slowly bent over to sit. *Move over chair*, I said to myself. And just as Headmistress Larriby's big ol' butt was about to hit the seat of the chair, it slid sharply to the left and she plopped to the floor with a big *BOOM!* Laughter erupted throughout the huge room as lopsided nostril-man struggled to pull her up.

Yeah, that was probably not the best time for my Monday power to work.

Chapter Eight

I ran to the front of the room to help Nostril-Man get Headmistress Larriby to her feet. I felt totally guilty.

"I guess stuff like this is the reason I'm here." I forced a laugh, trying to joke with her in hopes of getting on her good side—if she had one at all, that is. I definitely didn't want to spend my first night in the "haunted forest." It couldn't really be haunted, right?

"Just take that seat over there." She pointed to a chair in the corner of the room that had magically appeared. Someone in the room was obviously a pretty good Monday.

"We will settle this later," she said harshly. The audience was quiet and stared until I reached the seat.

Settle this later? I didn't even want to think about what that could mean.

"Welcome to the fiftieth summer session at Power Academy." She paused, awaiting some sort of applause, but the only one clapping was nostril-man. And clapping he was … way too vigorously. In fact, his slicked-back gray hair moved a bit. Ick.

"Let's get going, shall we?" Larriby said. I hated it when adults have that lofty, *I'm so smarter and wiser than you* kind of tone where they ask a question, but don't really expect an answer. Did she really think that we were waiting in excited anticipation for her to speak?

"Most summers you are grouped by weekday," she said, pushing Nostril-Man to the side. Apparently, he was invading her space. His shoulders slumped. She cleared her throat and continued. "For example, Mondays would be grouped together, Wednesdays would, Thursdays, and so on."

I was pretty sure we could figure out what she meant by *grouped by weekday*.

"This year, however, you will be grouped in a different manner." When she said those last words I could have sworn her eyes darted from Logan, to Ellie, to me, and then landed somewhere in the back of the room.

"*Oohs*" and "*Ahhs*" escaped from the crowd.

"Hush," Headmistress Larriby spat.

Silence.

"This year you will be grouped in teams of four. It

works out perfectly that there will be two girls and two boys on each team."

The crowd began mumbling.

"Sarah, be my partner," I heard a whisper from the lanky Wednesday in front of me. I watched this supposed Sarah as she nodded in agreement.

A lot of similar murmurs spread throughout the echoing room.

"Do you actually think I will let you choooose your own group?" the snarkiness in Mrs. Larriby's voice shut everyone up in an instant. "Each group will consist of one Monday, one Wednesday, one Thursday, and one Friday, as it's important to know how your powers can work together. To be sure you can work together in the real world, that is." She did those air quote thingies when she said "real world."

I caught Logan's eye and frowned. Chances were, we wouldn't be in the same group. Ellie flicked her hair again, and bumped into his shoulder. Was she flirting? That would be typical friend-stealing Ellie. Not that I was jealous or anything.

"I have posted the groups and coordinating dorm rooms on the bulletin board in the entrance hall," Mrs. Larriby bellowed.

My palms began to sweat. Gosh. I really hoped that I wouldn't be stuck with Ellie. If so, I would totally change it.

"The room assignments are final, and may NOT be

altered." Mrs. Larriby looked directly at me as she said this. I felt a lump begin to form in my throat as I realized that she must be a Thursday and just read my mind. Did I miss that information in the brochure?

Nostril-man stood on his tiptoes and whispered something into her ear. "Ah ... fine," she said with her eyebrows creased in frustration.

"Attention, all. This gentleman would like to be introduced," Headmistress Larriby said this with utter disgust. "This is my assistant, Mr. Grimeley." She pulled him toward her so he was now standing in the center of the stage. I further examined his outfit and noticed that just like Larriby, he wasn't much of a dresser (not that I'm a fashion expert or anything—I leave that up to Veronica). His too-long pants rolled over the top of his shoes, and there was actually another patch of gray hair on the top of his head. I neglected to see the pants thing earlier because I couldn't keep from staring at his nose and the giant caterpillar that peeked out.

"Hello," he said in a high squeaky voice that took me a little off guard. "I am Mr. Grimeley." He paused and his eyes darted around the room. Even from where I sat, I could see sweat beading at the top of his head. "And ... I ... I ..." He swallowed hard. "I will be leading you all in your one-on-one group check-ins."

His eyes immediately darted down at his covered feet

as he shuffled back to the platform. He obviously wasn't moving fast enough because Mrs. Larriby helped him out by shoving his scrawny body out of the way and behind her.

"The check-ins will occur every other day," she took over, menacingly looking at Mr. Grimeley. "Mr. Grimeley will meet with you to assess the progress you make in your weekday power. If you have not mastered your power to a certain degree by the end of the summer, then you will be joining us again next year." As she spoke the last line, she smirked and revealed yellow teeth that appeared extra banana-ey yellow against her puke-colored dress.

Her fat arm lifted. "Now go to the hall, find your team assignment, and then get to your rooms. Lights out at twenty-thirty." I did the math in my head. Eight-thirty.

Mr. Grimeley pointed his knobby finger toward the large oak doors, and they flew open instantly. Apparently, that was our cue to leave.

I looked toward where Logan was sitting and found an empty chair. Ellie probably grabbed him to go along with her. I was pushed out the door with the frenzied crowd. Everyone surrounded the bulletin board in one massive clump. I heard "yes" and "oh, man," and girls and boys were jumping around hugging one another after seeing their placements. I hoped that I would be so happy.

After the crowd had died down a bit, I made my way

to the team assignment list and saw a boy wearing a giant cowboy hat staring at it. Light emitted from his index finger running down the paper, trying to find his name. He turned around and pushed his black-rimmed glasses up his nose. "I don't know any of those people," he complained sadly, and shrugged. Poor Wednesday. But he seemed like a pretty decent one if he could light the sheet up like that.

Quickly, I tried to get him out of the way so I could read over the list before the few stragglers lagging behind got there first. Unsuccessful.

I looked in Pickle's den. "Can't I catch a break?" I asked. She yawned and curled up so that her body formed a furry circle.

"I told you we would settle this later." Headmistress Larriby's voice came from behind. With a yellow grin as big as the moon she added, "Enjoy your roommate." She spun on her heels and went into her office. Mr. Grimeley shuffled behind like a lost puppy. He caught my gaze and shook his head.

I rushed over to the list, and pushed the few students out of the way. I was breathing pretty hard at this point.

TEAM 5

Poppy Mayberry

Samuel Bricker

Logan Prince

And then I saw it. The reason I was sure Mrs. Larriby was smiling so yellow-moon-brightly. The last member of my team and my roommate for the entire, miserable, hate-my-life summer.

Ellie Preston

Chapter Nine

"You know that this is totally your fault?" Ellie shouted, claiming the bed next to the window by throwing her pink paisley designer duffle bag on top of it. "I mean, the only reason we are roomed together is because of that idiotic chair stunt you pulled with Larriby. If you would just—"

"It wouldn't hurt you to be a little nicer to me, you know?" I cut her off and sat down on my lopsided bed. Great. I let Pickle out of her purple traveling den, and she ran laps around the room. She knew enough to stay out of Ellie's way, though.

Ellie began unpacking her bag and shoved pink shirt after pink shirt into the larger dresser next to the door. She claimed that, too. She "huffed" and "puffed" every time a drawer slammed shut as if it were the worst thing in the world to be tasked with. I guess she was used to others unpacking belongings for her. Spoiled little Thursday brat.

"Heard that." She turned toward me and rolled her eyes for like the *bajillionth* time since we arrived just two hours ago.

Stupid mind-reading Thursday brat, I thought on purpose.

"And why did you have to bring that annoying little dog?" She glared at Pickle.

No one in their right mind could possibly think that Pickle was an annoying little dog. In fact, she rarely barks and is so well-trained and behaved that she's the total opposite of annoying. Why couldn't Ellie see that? Everyone who meets Pickle practically loves her. I mean, just look at that cute little face.

"Seriously? Why couldn't you just bring a hamster or fish or something?" she continued while unpacking what seemed to be the last shirt from her Mary-Poppins-deep bag. She had like three more to unpack yet, and one was bound to be filled with shoes.

And then she opened the next bag. I laughed inside. Bingo! Shoes.

"Or why not jewelry?" Ellie pranced toward me. Pickle yapped. "Shush up, Peanut." She kicked her pedicured foot forward, and my precious puppy cowered back.

"Her name's Pickle," I corrected Ellie. At least Ellie got the "P" right. I bent down and scratched Pickle behind her ear. She whined in approval.

"Whatever." Ellie looked toward her wrist. "For *my* personal belonging, I brought this bracelet that my mother got me for Christmas." She used her other hand to twirl it around her wrist right in front of my face. "There are twelve charms in all. White gold." She stood up straighter and shook her head so that her hair lay perfectly in place, and then walked back to her side of the room, took off the bracelet, and gingerly placed it into a tiny pink jewelry box. "A bit nicer than that chunk of orange rock you keep around your neck," she mumbled.

I pretended to ignore the last comment and watched as she glanced down at Pickle who was now licking the fur over her front paw. "Yep, you should have just brought a fancy piece of jewelry or something." She shrugged. "But I guess you probably don't have anything fancy at all," she said. Her eyes scanned me up and down like they did to Logan just a few hours earlier. But with me, the look could kill.

This girl was crazy. Could she not realize that Pickle was worth a heck of a lot more to me than some stupid piece of jewelry? And who was she to give me any advice about what I should have brought as *my* personal belonging?

"And maybe you should try finding your own friends

for once," I said without thinking, and sort of wished that I could have taken it back.

"What? Are you jealous of me and your new *boyfriend* or something?" she asked sarcastically and laughed.

One, I could definitely only see Logan as a friend. Hello? I hadn't even had a crush on anyone—yet. Two, I could never be jealous of Ellie. And three, this had not been the first time Ellie had attempted to take a friend from me. Celia Green and I were best friends through third grade until—

I could see Ellie giving me the *I'm reading your mind again* stare.

"Or are you still upset over Celia totally dissing *you* to be *my* Bff?" Her voice was getting more and more irritating to me.

I could have come back and said some nasty stuff right back to her then and there, but I'm not a malicious person like Ellie. Plus, I realized that I was going to be trapped with this stuck-up girl all summer, so no matter how much we insulted each other and brought up all that drama from the past, I was ... well ... stuck. Mrs. Larriby said that all room assignments were final, and I definitely did NOT want to cross her anymore after that whole chair incident. So really, I needed to make the best of this situation and try to fix whatever problem Ellie had with me.

I cleared my throat. "Ellie?"

I could tell by her sigh that she was annoyed. "Yes,

Poppy?" she asked, batting her eyelashes, emphasizing the "Ps."

"Why do you hate me? 'Cause if it's over that whole headband thing like forever ago, you just have to know that I totally did not mean for that to happen."

Well, I kind of did want that to happen. But I was trying to make amends. And here I was finally getting up the nerve to confront her, and she wouldn't even answer.

So I just kept on talking. "I mean, you were *never* actually nice to me, but especially the last year or so, you have been just ..." I paused as her eyes burned into mine. "Just downright cruel." I took a breath, happy that I was able to get it out. And then I leaned back and grabbed Pickle, afraid of how Ellie might react if she were to yap at her again.

Ellie sat down on her bed directly across from me and held my gaze. Her tone changed. "It's not that I ever really *hated* you," she muttered. She looked away, and then pursed her lips like she does when Mr. Salmon forces her to answer a tough math question when he knows she hasn't been reading his mind.

"You just ..."

I may have actually been getting through to her.

"You just ... never mind. You're so annoying." She stood up and pulled out her lollypop-red nail polish, and began painting away. "We just need to *tolerate* each other this summer. Stay out of my way, and I'll stay out of yours," she demanded, the softness in her voice gone.

I looked around at the tiny room that was more like a ten-by-twelve box, and decided that staying out of each other's way might be a little more difficult than it seemed.

When I woke up the next morning, I forgot where I was for a minute. I stared up at the ceiling and didn't see the glow-in-the-dark stick-on stars that my dad and I carefully placed last summer. This ceiling was painted an ugly shade of green (kind of similar in color to Headmistress Larriby's dress from yesterday). The chipped-off paint on the walls revealed the same floral wallpaper as the entrance hall downstairs.

It smelled a little off, too. My room at home almost always smells like fresh laundry—with the laundry room just a few feet away. But the room here at Power Academy smelled like a mixture of dust and cat litter. I only knew the smell of cat litter because we used to have a cat named Princess Flufferpie, until I found out that I was allergic to her. A while after giving Princess Flufferpie away, Pickle showed up on our doorstep one Halloween dressed as a ... well ... pickle.

Pickle licked the side of my face and brought me back to the reality and the ugliness that was Power Academy. I looked over to my left and saw Ellie still fast asleep. She actually looked kind of human then—not like her usual, nasty self. Her freshly painted hand dangled over the side of the bed. I looked up to see her mouth hanging wide open, and laughed at the fact that light breathy snores escaped from her lips.

Swish, swish. Two pieces of paper slid under the door. I tiptoed over to them in my purple fuzzy slippers and swooped them up. Our daily schedules. I clicked on my bedside light and scanned over them quickly to see that I have pretty much the same classes every day. Not as scary as I had imagined.

Poppy Rose Mayberry: Monday
Team 5
Room 205

8:15-9:00	— Breakfast
9:15-11:00	— History of Nova 101
11:00-11:15	— Break
11:15-1:00	— Monday Power Intensive (Power Boot Camp)

1:15- 2:00	— Lunch
2:15- 4:00	— Team Practice (M-W-F)
	— Team Meeting With Mr. Grimeley (T/TH)
4:00-6:00	— Monday Power Practice (with Power-Intensive group)
6:00-7:00	— Dinner
7:00-8:00	— Dorm Room
8:30	— Lights Out

I sneaked a quick glance at Ellie's and saw that she had the same exact schedule as me. Except hers said Thursday Power Intensive class instead of Monday. Practically with her all. Day. Long. Ugh.

"Well, Pickle. That's just fantastic," I whispered and showed her the schedules. She let out a whimper, obviously commiserating with me.

I froze, noticing the rustling in Ellie's bed. I was not ready to deal with her awake self yet. She rolled over on her side. Whew!

After dressing for the day in the spacious shared bathroom I quietly sneaked back into my room. Pickle was cuddled up against my pillow. Ellie's snoring was getting louder and louder. Seven-forty-five. Even though I probably should have woken her up so she was ready for breakfast, I decided not to. The quiet was nice.

I leafed through my *History of Nova* textbook, and got

bored of it in like two seconds. I petted Pickle, and got tired of that like two more seconds later. There wasn't any homework yet, so that wasn't an option. And, it's not like I could have called Veronica (not that she would've been up that early anyway). What was I thinking? I love to read and I didn't even bring a book. So, I decided to just practice my power. What harm could that have done in that little room?

My goal was to float Ellie's schedule a few measly feet across the room and land on her nightstand. I concentrated really hard on it and imagined it gently lifting into the air. It happened. Okay. Great. I continued concentrating on it until it was about six inches off of the comforter.

Then I willed it to slowly float over to her nightstand. My eyes and finger followed the paper as it moved horizontally and toward the right place. Awesome. This was sooo awesome!

Why was I even at Power Academy?

And that's when it all went wrong. As the schedule passed over Ellie's head, it swooped down and swiped the center of her face.

"Ouch," she screamed, and sat up so fast I thought her retainer (yes, retainer, she is human after all) was going to fly out of her mouth.

I cringed as she pulled it from her teeth, and a stream of slobber followed behind. Gross-fest! Her other hand cupped her nose.

"What the heck were you doing?" she squealed, reaching on her nightstand for the light, and then for a mirror. "Look at what you did." Her hand pointed to the tip of her nose.

Squinting, I leaned forward, trying to see what she was pointing at, but saw nothing.

"Don't you see it?" she asked, still pointing.

I took a step toward her and stared at her nose some more. Finally, I thought I could see it—a teeny tiny paper cut, barely even noticeable to the naked eye.

"Sorry, Ellie. I was just practicing."

"Yeah, right! Just you wait until I tell Headmistress Larriby about this," she said while dabbing the scratch with a piece of tissue. Really?

"I was just trying to get the schedule to your nightstand without waking you up. I swear," I pleaded.

Ellie sighed and reached for the pink robe draped over the foot of her bed. She threw it on over her pajamas, grabbed her Caboodle toiletry kit, and charged to the door. "What-ev," she shouted, slamming the door behind.

Obviously, I couldn't do anything right.

Chapter Ten

I was happy to find Logan sitting alone in the cafeteria for two reasons. For one, it was nice to see a friendly face instead of a scowl from Ellie. And two, it was a relief that I didn't have to be *that* girl who eats by herself in the corner.

"Thanks for totally abandoning me yesterday," I said, cracking a smile as I set down my tray of blueberry pancakes. I was really only half-serious in saying this.

"Sorry about that," he said with sincerity. "Ellie's like a cling-on, and I couldn't get rid of her." His eyes rolled. "I can see how she annoys you."

I smiled. He called her a cling-on and she annoyed him. "Is it that obvious?"

He gave me an *of course it's obvious* look. "Yeah."

Logan was definitely perceptive.

"Hey, Logan," a boy with hair as red as mine and my Mom's (I missed her), freckles, and frameless glasses plopped down next to Logan. Even without the giant cowboy hat, I recognized him as the Wednesday from last night with the light-up finger.

"This is Sam Bricker."

"Ah … the Wednesday that completes our group."

"Yep. That's me," he said, pushing the too-large glasses up his tiny freckled nose.

"So, I guess you're home-schooled too?" I asked, taking a bite of syrup-soaked super tasty pancake.

"Nah. I'm already at Nova Middle." He dropped his head to his chin. "Repeater P.A. student this summer."

"It looked like you were using your light power pretty well last night," I said, confused, thinking about how his hand so effortlessly lit up to scan the assignment list.

He shrugged and pushed up his glasses. "I *am* pretty good with it, that's the problem." He looked around the cafeteria and then leaned in forward and over the table. His lips curved into a mischievous smirk. "The last day of P.A. last summer, I was kind of responsible for that whole power outage thing."

I knew exactly what incident he was talking about. Just about everyone in Nova knew about it. Veronica's cousin's friend told Veronica, and then she told me, that

Headmistress Larriby made one of the students so upset that he made the power go out during the P.A. graduation ceremony. There was no electricity for two days because of it and Larriby and her strange sidekick had to find another place to stay. I had never heard of a Wednesday doing anything that big with their power. Not even my dad could do something like that.

But looking at the freckled, baby-faced Wednesday sitting across from me, I could hardly believe that he would do something like that at all. This little geeky guy was a total rebel troublemaker—and obviously a heck of a good Wednesday.

For the rest of breakfast we talked about school, friends, and our family. We also came to the conclusion that if all of Power Academy's food tasted like those pancakes, maybe we didn't want to go home at the end of the summer. Thinking of Headmistress Larriby made us second-guess that conclusion, though.

Based on personalities (not powers, because I still needed to get better at mine), we made a pretty decent trio. It was just too bad Ellie had to be part of our Team Five. We saw that we all had the same first class: Nova Power History 101 and walked there together.

I didn't really understand how learning about Nova's history for like the millionth time would help me and all the other captive prisoners in developing our powers, but we were forced to take it anyway.

"Logan, you read first." Mrs. Barkdoll's voice was muffled by the seating chart practically shoved up her nose. She could have really used some glasses.

Logan scooted his chair closer to his desk and began.

"It was in 1954 when the first meteor crashed directly into the center of Nova that the first power was discovered. It was a Monday; Roy Lichtenberg woke up to find that—"

And that's where I drifted off. Not that I didn't want to hear about my city's history (yet again), it's just that all that sci-fi stuff totally bored me. So, instead of listening, I wrote my first note to Veronica.

> *BFF Veronica,*
> *Save me.*
> *Xoxo, Poppy*

Short and swee—

"You're up next, Miss Mullberry," Mrs. Blind-as-a-Bat Barkdoll's sharp voice came from directly above my head. I assumed she was talking to me, even though she got my name wrong.

"I … uh …" I stuttered. I had no idea where Logan left off. I shot a look his way to see if he could give me a hint.

"Fourteen," I swore I heard him whisper, but didn't think his mouth moved. Strange.

I rapidly turned to page fourteen and smiled up at Mrs. Barkdoll. She probably couldn't tell I changed my facial expression at all.

"Miss Mullberry," she said again. "Are you just about ready?"

Mullberry? Really?

I glanced at the page enough to notice it was the right one, but I had no idea exactly where he left off. My heart started to race a little faster. How embarrassing to completely zone out the first day of class. I would never get out of this place alive at this rate.

But then I was saved by the least likely person.

"Don't start without me," Ellie's obnoxious (and nasally) voice drifted from the back of the room. All heads turned to see her standing in the frame wearing one of her many pink T-shirts and a white skirt. Her right hand covered her nose. Drama Queen.

"I am sooo terribly sorry for being late. I had to rush to the nurse's office for a little emergency." Ellie's eyes narrowed and shot to mine. She clacked her way to the center of the classroom and removed her hand from her face, revealing a thumb-sized Band-Aid spread across her nose.

Half the class gasped.

Really? Was that really necessary? Again, drama queen!

"Over there, Miss," she squinted at the class roster,

"Miss Prescott, is it?"

"Preston," Ellie emphasized, smiling. The class chuckled. "Ellie Preston." Her laser-whitened teeth were practically blinding.

Mrs. Barkdoll pointed to an empty chair next to Sam. *Is this Ellie?* he mouthed to me and grinned from ear to ear. I nodded.

"Now I forget where we left off," Mrs. Barkdoll admitted.

Ellie raised her hand. "I'll begin."

Phew! Dodged that one.

The fifteen-minute break between classes was definitely needed. I ran upstairs and spent a little time with Pickle. When I got into the room, she immediately dropped a stuffed toy rabbit from her mouth and greeted me. Her tail wagged back and forth faster than my eyes could see.

"This is gonna be a looooong summer, Picks." I grabbed one of her favorite peanut-butter treats and tossed it right into her mouth. "But I'm so glad to have you with me."

Her furry head leaned into my hand as I gave her one last scratch behind her ears. I shut the door and heard her whines behind it. Poor girl hated to see me leave. I couldn't even begin to imagine how she would have felt if I had left her behind in Nova. Sure, she was our *family* dog, but everyone knew she was really mine.

I headed back downstairs to the Monday room for my Monday Power Intensive class. I slipped through the huge wooden door just as it began to shut.

"Take your seat," a super tall, skinny young woman with white-blond hair slicked back in a tight ponytail said. Her tiny index finger moved up and down and up and down. Just like the rest of the Mondays in there, my eyes were locked on the chalk that was suspended midair, writing on the board clear on the other side of the room. She was good.

Welcome, Mondays!
Miss Maggie

We continued to stare in awe as the chalk flew over our heads and into her petite hand. I couldn't wait until I could do stuff like that.

"Welcome to the Monday Power Intensive class," she said with an awesome British accent. Because of the accent alone, I could tell I liked her already.

Sometimes Veronica and I would spend days pretending that we're British. She was the Pippa to my Kate. We'd go to the mall and say things like "cheerio!" (goodbye), "knickers" (underwear), and "chim-chimity." Well, maybe that last one was Mary Poppins. We just like talking that way—even if people look at us funny.

But I wondered how Miss Maggie got that accent. I mean, most people who are from Nova stay in Nova. She must have moved out of this place early in life and picked it up.

First Miss Maggie read over the rules for her class. They were pretty much the same as the rules at school, except when she talked about leaving to use the bathroom she said "the loo" instead. Loved it!

Then she went through the list of other Mondays and asked us to tell her about the progress of our powers.

A tiny girl with light brown hair and tan skin named Olive Pittman sat next to me. She admitted that she has never been able to move a single thing without using her hands. Her complete lack of skills totally made me feel confident in my uncontrollable ones.

"Charlie Fillman, and I don't want to learn about my stupid power," a boy with super curly brown hair spoke from the back of the room with his arms crossed over his chest. He propped his feet on the back of the chair in front of him and huffed. Miss Maggie just smiled.

And the four other Mondays took their turns. Three of them were a set of triplets named Tara, Tina, and Telia. "Our parents don't like us to practice in the house," they said simultaneously, and later admitted that meant they didn't practice their Monday powers at all.

The last Monday was a girl named Matilda with dark skin and black hair. From just a quick glance, I thought that she might be shorter than even me.

"Some days I'm on, and some days I'm off," she said in a squeaky voice I would expect to come from a mouse. A friendly smile beamed from her face.

Miss Maggie used her telekinesis to bring my schedule to her. Her straight white teeth smiled at me. "Ahhnd, you must be Popp-ay."

"Yes, I do believe so," I said in a half-British, half-American accent. What the heck was I doing? The other Mondays giggled as I slinked back in my chair. But Miss Maggie smiled warmly, almost like we were friends.

"The purpose of this class is to … well … improve upon your Monday powers." At that moment Miss Maggie pointed to a long blue desk with seven glasses filled with water lined up in a row.

"This is your first assignment." She motioned us toward the desk.

"This should be fun," Matilda squealed. A ginormous smile spread across her face. Now that she was standing next to me, I could see that I was right earlier. She was super short and came just to my chin.

"Your goal is to get the glass of water from the desk and into your hands. *Only* using your Monday power. Like this."

Miss Maggie's bright blue eyes stared at the glass on the end. She pointed her index finger out straight as an arrow. The glass lifted effortlessly into the air, floated ever so delicately, and landed in her hand. She sent it back and it came back down silently on the table.

"You're really good at that," Matilda said, wide-eyed, slapping her hands together in approval.

"Years of practice." Miss Maggie nodded. "Matilda, why don't you try first?"

Miss Maggie moved her slender frame out of the way and Matilda took her place.

"Now concentrate extremely hard. You need to block out all distractions and just picture that glass," (sounded like gloss) "of water landing ever so delicately into your hands."

I could see the intense look coming from Matilda's brown eyes. She was totally focused. The glass wobbled a bit at first and then slowly lifted from the desk. Not two seconds later it came crashing back down on the table. Water spilled everywhere.

"DUCK!" Miss Maggie yelled as a roll of paper towels

flew above our heads and into her hands.

"I'm so sorry," Matilda said frowning.

"It's perfectly all right. You will learn in time," Miss Maggie assured her, using her telekinesis to clean up the mess. She pointed to the trashcan next to her desk, and in another swift motion the lid popped open and in dropped the wet towels. "Three Ts, you're up next."

Tara, Tina, and Telia stood in a line. After what seemed like an hour of scrunched faces and goofy grunting noises, none of their glasses of water even budged an inch. Those poor triplets.

"Perhaps we shall try another day," Miss Maggie said, and smiled warmly at them. I couldn't believe how awesome she was, not at all like I had imagined the power "boot camp" teacher to be like. This was the class where I heard horror stories of dodging softballs and controlling the throwing of knives. Yikes. Gotta love Veronica and her exaggerations.

"Okay, Poppy. Now, it's your turn."

My hands immediately clammed up, but I felt a little bit better when I looked over to see Matilda's enthusiastic eyes and wide smile. I could tell that she totally wanted me to do well. All three "T" triplets stared at me in wonder, as if I were about to eat the world's largest hamburger or attempt something crazy like that. Charlie Fillman still sat in the back of the room, unmoved. In fact, his eyes were closed and I was pretty sure—

Swish. The paper-towel roll flew over our heads again and landed on Charlie. He snorted as his head darted up. We all giggled.

Miss Maggie acted as if she had no idea where that paper-towel roll came from. "Now, nice and slow," she said, drawing the attention back to me.

Just like Miss Maggie had said earlier, I blocked out everyone around me until they were all just blurs in my peripheral vision. I heard a few whispers from behind, but tuned them out too. I concentrated on that end glass alone. *Lift. Lift. Lift.* It began to wobble a bit, and just when I thought it was about to tip over, it lifted into the air.

"Oohs" and *"Ahhs"* came from behind me, but I concentrated on keeping that glass suspended.

I heard Miss Maggie's heels click and clack as she walked toward me, but didn't let that distract me either. "Now will it forward," she whispered.

"Go forward, go forward, go forward," I quietly said to myself. And just like that, the glass listened. It was suspended midair. Awesome! This was so awesome!

"Just a little bit farther, Poppy. Now reach out to grab it."

I slowly reached out my other hand. "Go to hand, go to hand, go to hand," I whispered. And then when I practically felt the cold glass against my sweating hot palms

... *CRASH*.

Darn it!

I had failed at the whole Monday thing once again.

The silence broke when someone started clapping. "You're amazing, Poppy!" Matilda squealed so enthusiastically I was almost convinced. "Closest one in the class!"

"So close, Poppy," Miss Maggie said and patted me on the back. "It seems that it may not take you long af—"

BEEP! Miss Maggie was cut off by the loud speaker, and then came Headmistress Larriby's urgent (and annoying) masculine voice. "Would the following students please report to the library immediately. Logan Prince. Samuel Bricker. Ellie Preston. And Poppy Mayberry."

Great. What did I do now?

Chapter Eleven

"Logan! Sam!" I shouted as they entered the library, motioning to two empty chairs next to me. "Over here."

"Over here, guys!" I heard Ellie yell from the other side of the room.

I turned around to see her arms vigorously waving. Ugh. And she had changed her outfit. In pink from head to toe, she looked like a skinny little flamingo trying to take off in flight. Logan looked at her, and then at me. He took the seat next to mine. I sent a friendly little smirk Ellie's way.

Sam took the seat next to her. By his reaction when she entered Nova History class, I kind of figured he would.

"What do you think this is about?" Logan asked.

I shrugged.

The door crashed behind us as Headmistress Larriby scuffled down the center aisle. She looked like a giant eggplant. Again, her too-tight purple dress hugged her body in all the wrong places, and she had a funny-looking poufy green scarf tied around her neck. I knew that was too tight, too, because a skin roll hung over it. Yuck.

Mr. Grimeley followed close behind. His hair was slicked down with so much gel that it looked like gray paint was melting off his head. I laughed inside a little.

Larriby stopped in the center of the room and positioned herself in what looked like a football tackle stance. Then she wedged a fat finger between the green fabric and her neck. The scarf must have been cutting off circulation. She cleared her throat. "It seems that we have had a security breach here at Power Academy," her manly voice boomed as if we were seated a mile back, rather than two feet in front of her.

"That's not our problem!" Sam retorted, wiping from his cheek a bit of talk-spit that flew out of Mrs. Larriby's matching eggplant-purple lipstick-stained mouth.

Headmistress Larriby took a step forward and stared at him coldly. She was in his face now. "Actually, Mr. Bricker, it *is* your problem." I chuckled again inside as more spittle flew from her lips and onto his face. Poor Sam. That was gross.

She took a step back and then addressed us all. "It seems that sometime over the course of today, someone gained access to your private rooms."

"I know I locked *my* door on the way out this morning," Ellie said, looking at me. The way she emphasized the *my* and neglected to acknowledge that the room belonged to me, too, kind of ticked me off.

Shoot! Did I lock the door after I went up there on break? I thought back and knew for a fact that I at least shut the door. But had I locked it? It would have been as simple as turning the little lock on the kno—

"You are unbelievable," Ellie said sharply, whipping her head toward me. Her whole Thursday mind-reading thing was getting on my nerves. "Ugh." She sighed, straightened her hair back out, and rolled her eyes. I determined at this point that the eye-rolling thing was pretty much her favorite facial gesture—especially regarding me.

"Whoever entered your rooms obviously wanted to get something personal to you," Mrs. Larriby continued while glancing quickly at Mr. Grimeley. "With that being said," she cleared her throat, "each of your *personal treasures* has been stolen." Right after Mrs. Larriby uttered those words, I swore there was smile forming on her face.

"Are you trying to tell me that someone stole my bracelet?" Ellie shrieked, fanning her hands in front of her face.

Mr. Grimeley handed Mrs. Larriby a sheet of paper. "I am saying, that someone stole not only that, but ..." She looked down at the tattered notebook in front of her. "A soccer ball."

"Hey! That was autographed!" Logan shouted.

"A clarinet." I assumed that it must have been Sam's. A cowboy hat and glasses-wearing-mischievous-clarinet-playing Wednesday. That boy was certainly full of surprises.

Headmistress Larriby's eyebrows curved in. "And a favorite ... pickle?" But Larriby phrased this last one more like a question than a statement and looked at me with disgust.

Before we came to Power Academy we had to send in an information form. The name of our one personal belonging had to be approved before we started classes for the summer, so they definitely knew what our items were. Well, kind of. Mine simply said pickle. Okay, so maybe I hadn't been quite clear on the information sheet about the fact that Pickle was kind of a living, furry, barking thing, not a cucumber-vinegar mixture. Whoops!

And then it sunk in. Pickle was missing. Gone. Someone had stolen her. I could very possibly never see her again.

But as terrible as it could be, and as upset as I should have been, I had a nagging feeling that something seemed off about this whole situation. Larriby was way too calm. If there were really some sort of person going around this academy stealing things, why wouldn't Larriby be more concerned?

"Ooookkaaay," Ellie shouted. "So, you're telling me that *my* bracelet is, like, gone for real and forever?" Ellie hyperventilated a little, just seconds away from tearing up.

"What are you gonna do about it?" Logan asked with eyes glaring at the two adults in front of us.

Shouldn't they have had the answer? They called us into this meeting in the first place.

Ellie reached into her jumbo purse. "I'm calling my mother," she said, pulling her pink rhinestone phone from it.

We all knew that cell phones weren't allowed. But it seemed that, once again, Ellie felt that she was the exception to the rule. Mr. Grimeley's hand flew up and his index finger pointed directly to the glittering phone. In a matter of seconds, it flew from Ellie's grasp and crashed into a bookcase. Hundreds of pink plastic flecks fell to the floor below like sparkly confetti. He was really good.

"My phone!" she cried.

"No one is calling anybody," Headmistress Larriby said. Actually, she more like demanded this. What the heck was going on?

Mr. Grimeley stepped forward. "This is getting a little out of hand," he whispered into Larriby's ear. Since we all could hear him, it wasn't really a whisper.

"Fine!" Her eyes again burned into his, and then they turned toward us. "I guess enough is enough," she said angrily, like this was entirely our fault or something.

We looked at one another, confused. Ellie's sobs died down to a few sniffles.

"Your items are safe and sound." Her creased face made it seem like she was in pain saying this. She liked toying with us. But this was good news for the four of us.

"Then why would you tell us they were stolen?" Sam stood up so forcefully his chair crashed backward. Two lamps on a reading desk flickered on and off a few times— he was not happy at all. None of us were.

Ellie's foot stomped not-so-delicately on the floor. "What is going on?" Her eyes darted over to what was left of her demolished phone.

"Yeah," we all said simultaneously. We wanted answers, and we wanted them now.

She motioned for everyone to sit back down. We hesitantly did. "While you all were in your Power Intensive classes this morning, Mr. Grimeley and I retrieved your items from your rooms."

Headmistress Larriby towered over me. A chunk roll was practically in my face. "I was unaware that Pickle was a measly little dog," she spat.

I thought about poor Pickle and how she would be without me.

Mrs. Larriby's eyes shot to me. "Oh, she's perfectly safe, Poppy. Stop obsessing," she said, brushing me off and reading my mind.

"Get to the point, please," Logan demanded, taking Larriby's attention away from me. Whew. I sent a thank-you smile his direction.

She gave a long hard sigh. "Let's just say, we want to give you all a chance to prove to us that you don't need to be here."

"Go on," Logan said, leaning forward. Some strands of hair fell into his face, and he brushed them away with the back of his hand. Part of me wanted to take a pair of scissors and just cut those hairs right off.

"Each year, we are *required* by Nova's Mayor Masters (nose-picking Mark's mom) to choose a group of Weekdays who we feel are already a bit ahead of the game." She rolled her eyes on the *required* part and then whispered something to Grimeley. I got the feeling that if it were up to Mrs. Larriby, no one would be given the chance to prove anything, and we would be stuck here with her forever.

"And?" Logan interrupted angrily.

Headmistress Larriby shot him the death stare. "And, as I said before, we are told to give you the opportunity to prove to us that you don't really need to be here." She looked back toward Mr. Grimeley and smirked. Her head whipped back around. "But it's up to *me*, as Power

Academy's head mistress, to decide *how* you prove that."

That explained the stealing of our stuff. Was that even legal?

"But why us?" Ellie asked, with her foot rapping quickly on the floor below.

Mrs. Larriby hesitantly looked at Mr. Grimeley once again. His eyes burned into hers as they made facial gestures back and forth. It was almost like they were communicating through their minds without the need for words or whispers. Strange.

The expressions on the faces of Ellie, Logan, and Sam told me that they caught the awkwardness too.

Finally, Mrs. Larriby sighed. "Poppy, your little, uh … What should I call it," she paused, "*display* on opening night told me you have potential," she said through a grimace.

I couldn't help but smile. Remembering Mrs. Larriby landing on her butt in front of everyone last night was priceless. And I was so close in my Monday class today that I knew I wasn't completely hopeless.

She looked toward Ellie. "I know you're only here because you take advantage of your power. Show me you can keep it under control and not use it ALL of the time."

Then she looked at Logan. "And, you, Mr. Prince. Let's put your little disappearing act to the test, shall we?"

To the test? What was she talking about?

"I came up with a little challenge." She smirked at Mr.

Grimeley once again. "Working together," she said, her fat finger wiggling back and forth between Ellie and me in particular, "and using your weekday powers, you have to find your precious little belongings, and bring them to me."

"How long do we have?" I asked.

"As long as it takes," she sneered, and then a sinister smile formed across her face. "The longer it takes, the longer you'll be stuck here. With me."

Ugh.

Sam used his Wednesday power and flicked the lights on and off a few more times. "What do you mean? As long as it takes." He imitated her manly voice on the last sentence.

"Exactly what I said. As. Long. As. It. Takes," she emphasized each word and glared at Sam. "If you can even find your precious belongings at all, that is."

I gulped.

"If you find your belongings and successfully return them to me and Mr. Grimeley here," at the mention of his name, Grimeley snorted and his nose hair forest wiggled, "you will have the opportunity to leave early." She paused and readjusted the scarf choking her neck. "That's a big IF!"

Her fat finger pointed to me. "I believe you'd like to be lounging around some pool with a certain friend of yours."

Ugh. Stupid Thursdays and their mind-reading power.

"And if we don't find the stuff?"

Mrs. Larriby smirked at Mr. Grimeley. "Then you're stuck at Power Academy for the rest of the summer, and you may even have to return next year." Her chin jiggled again as she let out a Wicked-Witch-of-the-West-like cackle and opened the door. "I have been forced to give a *promising* group of students this opportunity for the last five years, and not *once* has anyone been able to leave early." She showed those revolting teeth to us and continued, "And I intend to keep it that way. I'll be keeping a close eye on you kids. Good luh-uh-ck," she sang sarcastically, and the door shut behind her wiggly butt.

Okay, that whole butt thing was pretty mean of me to have thought, but I felt completely justified. That was one nasty woman.

It was then that I realized that Ellie was not the one to hate—Headmistress Larriby was. And we would show her.

I turned to my team. "Let's do this."

Chapter Twelve

Ellie literally threw her purse as hard as she could on the bed. Lip gloss, nail polish, a nail file, and the debris that was once her cell phone flew out and all over her pink duvet cover. "How does that ... that ... woman expect us to work through our classes, master our powers, and find our stuff?" she asked, fuming so much I swear smoke was about to blow out of her ears. I imagined that actually happening and chuckled.

"I guess we just have to come up with a plan."

During my last classes of the day, all I could think about was the challenge Headmistress Larriby proposed. I'd been trying to get a plan together all afternoon, but knew that we needed help from the boys.

Ignoring my plan suggestion, Ellie rustled through

her bag full of nail polish and grabbed out an awful arrest-me-now yellow bottle. "I mean, really? Who does that woman think she is?" she asked, painting away and totally missing her fingernails in the process. "I even wonder if Mayor Masters knows that this is the way she *challenges* her students. Hiding our stuff? And the first week, no less! Really? Wait until I tell my father!" She slammed the nail polish down on her dresser. "That woman just likes to torment people. Unbelievable!" she rambled.

I just let her vent. Her thoughts were pretty much the same as mine. For all I knew, she was reading them right out of my head. But even though I had ideas flying all around up there at like a million miles a minute, I seemed totally calm compared to the uber-stressed, red-faced Ellie. Pickle was at stake, not some inanimate object like, say, an expensive silly bracelet, so I needed to stay focused. Plus, BFF Veronica and I had that awesome summer planned. We needed to figure out where our things were and get the heck out of this messed-up Power Academy. There was no time to act crazy-stressed.

"So let's start brainstorming," I said, surprisingly levelheaded, and grabbed a notebook and my favorite purple pen from the tote at the foot of the bed sitting right next to Pickle's travel den. Poor Pickle was probably lost without me.

Ellie put the cap back on the polish and blew at her

fingertips. In a matter of minutes, her face had gone from fire engine red to a light pink hue. That whole nail-painting thing must be pretty therapeutic for her.

"Old Lady Larriby said that we need to work together as a group, so we should probably get the guys over here like A-sap," she said while blowing on her fingernails.

"You know the rules, though. No boys in a girl's room and no girls in a boy's room."

We made eye contact and nodded in agreement just like we read each other's minds. Rules or no rules, we needed their help. We had to get to them. Plus, Headmistress Larriby said that we had to prove ourselves while working together. Not apart. How would she expect us to do that *without* being together?

I glanced at the bright red flashing clock and saw that it was a little after eight-thirty. That meant that it was dorm-room time. If we quietly sneaked out now, more than likely no one would see us on the guys' floor. But we had to be real careful about not getting caught. Ugh. This would have been much easier if Ellie and I were invisible Fridays.

"Okay, Ellie, I have a plan." I walked over to her bed and moved the rest of the stuff that fell from her purse out of the way. She actually helped me make room.

"Thanks," I muttered, shocked by her kind gesture.

"What-ev," she said, pushing all hints of kindness away. "Do you think Mrs. Larriby is listening in on our thoughts right now?" I whispered.

"There's no way she could hear." Her eyes spastically bounced around the room. "Except, of course, if the room is bugged."

My eyes darted around then, too. "I think we're okay," I said, satisfied with my quick scan.

She pushed her hair behind her ears. Two yellow paint streaks stood out against her dark brown locks.

The giggle came out before I could even stop it.

She sighed. "For our Thursday power to work right, you have to be within like ten feet of the person whose mind you're reading. So, there's no way Old Lady Larriby can hear what we're up to from way down there in her office." She smirked. And for once, that smirk wasn't intended for me. "So, what's the plan?"

I leaned away from her, satisfied that no one else could hear our conversation. "Even though we don't know which room Logan and Sam are in, we know it is one of the eight on the first floor."

Ellie nodded and remained quiet, listening to my plan. It was nice to have her actually listen to me for once.

We made it down the main staircase with no problems. At the base of the stairs we had a perfect view of Headmistress Larriby in her office. She was bent over her desk with her big back toward us. Grrr. What the heck was she doing in there so late anyway? All she would have had to do was turn around and we would totally be trapped.

I thought about the P.A. handbook we got in the mail a few weeks ago …

Any student found fraternizing outside of their own dorm room after eight o' clock will face serious consequences. In addition, any student found fraternizing in a room belonging to the opposite sex will face serious consequences. Punishments could include meal isolation or being locked in the dorm room after socializing hours.

Prison.

Nevertheless, we were going to do this.

I caught Ellie's eye and pointed to my head.

She got the signal. *On three*, I thought. *One … two … three.* We ran across the large foyer and made it to the downstairs dorm hall without any problems. Headmistress Larriby had no clue. Ellie and I laughed together. Kind of like how friends would.

"Uck. Not even close to friends," she spat.

That hurt. Pushing her remark from my mind I said, "Start listening."

Ellie pressed her ear against the first door on the right. "Nope." Then the second. "Nope, again." And then the third. "Nope."

So much for the whole third time's a charm thing.

We got to the fourth door and she gave me thumbs-up. *I think I hear Sam*, she mouthed. And then I swore she said something about camouflage and reindeer, but I was pretty sure her mouth didn't move. Weird.

I balled my hand into a fist, and just as I was about to put it against the door, we both froze. Footsteps. No, more like drag-steps. Definitely the pants-over-shoes shuffling of greasy Mr. Grimeley.

I gave the door three quick raps. *Open it, open it, open it.* Ellie's ear was still pressed against the door. "Just a minute," Sam said.

Mr. Grimeley's footsteps got closer and louder. Only a few more feet to go, and he would turn the corner and catch us. There was no way we could ruin our chances of going home early before the first week was even up.

Just as the drag-steps were about to turn into the hall, the boys' door flew open and some unseen force propelled me forward. I bumped into Ellie as we both stumbled inside.

Sam was sitting in the dark, using his finger to read some hunting magazine. That explained the camo comment Ellie had made. Or I thought she made. Again, that boy continued to surprise me. A hunter now?

Ellie's eyes scurried around the room. "Where's Logan?"

"He went looking for you guys," Sam answered, still engrossed in his magazine.

Ellie looked at me with a totally puzzled expression. I smiled and didn't say a thing, thinking about that unforeseen force that pushed us into the room.

"We like definitely would have passed him if he were looking for us," Ellie said.

I spun around. "I know you're here, Logan," I teased. And just like that, Logan reappeared in front of our eyes. He was even better with his powers than I thought. That would definitely help our chances.

"Had the same idea as you girls." He smirked, plopped down next to Sam, and pushed hair out of his bright eyes that were looking directly into mine. For some reason I felt my cheeks grow warm as I smiled back.

I was in the room for about ten seconds, which was long enough to notice that it smelled like ... well ... boy. Instead of the sweet (sarcastic) smell of nail polish, dust, and cat litter, this room reeked of sweat and socks. And we had only been here a day. Gross. Boys are just ... gross ... most of the time at least. And how the heck did they already have a two-foot high pile of dirty laundry in the corner? Boys.

Ellie and I sat down on Logan's bed. The guys were facing us. There was this kind of weird silence as we just stared. I had never been in such a tiny space with boys. Without an adult around that is. And we were really breaking P.A. rules.

Logan took the initiative and stood up. "So, let's get started," he said abruptly and almost a little too drill-sergeant-like while clapping his hands in our faces.

Ellie and I flinched backward, looked at each other, and laughed. Heart beat still—that was like the second time today we actually laughed as if we were semi-acquaintances.

She rolled her eyes.

"We all have had a glimpse of that old meanie clothes-too-tight Larriby," Logan said. I snorted. It was cute that he used silly little nicknames to recognize people like I do. Did I just say cute? I meant to say nice. It was nice.

Ellie smirked at me.

"She probably has all our stuff locked up somewhere on campus." Logan paused, and turned toward Sam. "You were here last year, did anyone say anything about this?"

Sam's blue eyes pulled away from the magazine and he scratched his orange puffy head. "I have no idea. In fact, I didn't even know about the stuff going missing. Like Larriby said, nobody has ever gotten to go home early, so why would people admit that they failed at her stupid little challenge?"

The bed shook as Ellie stood up and started to pace. "I *need* that bracelet back. What if we can't find the stuff? Will that fashion-challenged, ugly, hateful woman actually keep them, like, forever?"

We all shrugged. No one could possibly know the answer. But, considering the way Headmistress Larriby had been treating us since we got here, she just might. That really scared me.

"What about Pickle? She's actually a living thing!" I said, thinking about how scared she must be without me. I could see it now. She was probably shaking uncontrollably in some dark corner of this prison just waiting for me to save her. Sure, Larriby told me she was safe, but how could I possibly know that for sure?

"Shut up about that stupid Peanut!" Ellie shouted, eyes burning into mind. "It's your own fault for bringing that furry little creature to Power Academy, anyway. And your fault we're even here because of that stupid chair stunt." She paced toward the door and dramatically whipped her head around so that her long hair went flying. "So maybe your stupid dog deserved to get taken!"

The room grew silent once again.

"That was pretty harsh, Ellie," Sam said, setting the magazine on his nightstand.

"Even for you," I sarcastically added, tentatively making eye contact with her—surprised that I'd even said it.

"Well, I'm *not* sorry," she said, breaking eye contact and gently sitting back down next to me.

Boy did she have a temper. Work together, huh? This was going to be one long summer.

Chapter Thirteen

So, while discussing our little challenge the next morning, we all decided that the best time, and only time, really, for us all to meet would be at dinner (which really wasn't the safest) and then during the dorm room time—which we would have to risk getting caught outside of our rooms.

Even though we had a time slot every other day for "Team" practice, it turned out that those sessions were held in the library and supervised by Headmistress Clothes-too-tight. She was probably going to do everything in her power to ensure we didn't find our missing items, so that would not be the best time to discuss our strategy—especially with her being a Thursday.

We also decided that each of us was going to have to work our butts off during our separate power-intensive classes. The better we mastered our powers, the more likely we could get our stuff back in the next few weeks. And the sooner we got our stuff, the sooner I would be lounging by the pool with Veronica sunbathing on one side of me and a big glass of cold lemonade on the other. I pictured Pickle in her cute purple-and-silver swimsuit and smiled. Mrs. Larriby said she was safe and sound, but I was super worried about her.

"Hey," Logan said, passing me with a tray of disgusting-looking food in his hands.

I turned my nose up and pointed to the dog-food-looking pile in front of him. "Is that what I think it is?"

He shoved a giant bite in his mouth. "If you're thinking of turkey and stuffing with gravy ... then yeah, that's exactly what this is." He took another bite right in my face and smiled. "Mmm ... I love Thanksgiving in summer," he said through chews.

I swallowed hard, trying not to look down at the tray of vomit-like food as he continued on to our table. Since you could choose either the prepared meal (turkey grossness) or the fresh fruit bar, it was easy to see that I would be having a banana with peanut butter for dinner, even though it's a little too healthy for my liking. Where's the mac-n-cheese and hotdogs when you need 'em?

I noticed that Ellie was going the healthier route as well. Wouldn't want to put a pound on that dainty little figure, now would we?

Ellie had uttered maybe a total of four sentences to me these first few days at Power Academy. Since her freak-out in the boys' room she still felt I was to blame for this whole challenge thing, and had been anything but nice. Her icy glares and blatant attempts at ignoring me were all the evidence I needed to know for sure that she hated me. The fact that we would never even come close to being friends was solidified. I just didn't get why she was so mean to me.

"So, what did you all find out?" Sam asked once we all got settled at the table.

Ellie pushed her plate of strawberries away and leaned in. I leaned away from her, but more importantly, from the stuffing. Yuck.

"I totally read my power teacher Mr. Brotwurst's mind. You know, just to see if he knew anything," she said, only making eye contact with Logan and Sam. It stung a little.

"Yeah?" Logan prompted.

Ellie sounded like she might have something good here.

"And …" Her eyes darted around, looking for any adults in the room. "It turns out that he is like totally a compulsive booger-eater."

This information had absolutely nothing to do with our mission. "What?" I asked, slightly annoyed.

"I know, gross, right?" Wide-eyed, she looked around at us (the boys) only to be greeted by dumbfounded expressions. "All he wanted to do all class was just reach up there and—"

"We get it," Logan cut her off.

The turkey stuffing was bad enough. Did we really have to discuss nose-picking and booger-eating? And I thought I had gotten away from people like Mark Masters—the nose-picking king of Nova.

Her shoulders slumped over. "Sorry. He just didn't think about anything useful for us. And you would think that in a room full of Thursdays he would censor his thoughts!"

I looked at the guys. "What about you two? Anything?"

They shrugged in unison.

"It doesn't seem like any of my teachers know a thing," said Sam. "But it's not like I can read minds or anything." He had this goofy smile on his face as he said this to Ellie.

I may not know much about flirting, but it seemed that Sam was totally making googly eyes at her. Better Ellie than me.

Logan shook his head. "Found nothing either."

We were so busy in my power intensive class starting with the basic stuff like moving feathers and lightweight objects that couldn't hurt anyone if they suddenly flew out of control (which mine did, bummer), that I didn't have the chance to talk to Miss Maggie about a thing. But I wasn't so sure she would know much of anything anyhow.

"Well, maybe, like, the teachers know about Larriby's

challenge, but they aren't allowed to say anything. You know?" Ellie said, quickly glancing at me, taking the words directly out of my head. Her cherry-ChapSticked lips curled into a smirk.

"She did say that we have to work together, so it would make sense for her to leave it completely up to us," I added, looking toward Ellie.

She stared at her fruit. So annoying! I should have given up on the whole trying to be nice to her thing. It was getting me nowhere.

"Yeah. Maybe Mr. Brotwurst thought about eating his boogers all day *because* he didn't want to give anything away through his thoughts," Logan added, taking a bite of stuffing. I cringed. How could he eat that? But he definitely had a point about Brotwurst's thoughts.

"Or maybe he just likes the taste of 'em," Sam added.

We all chuckled. Grossfest all the way!

"Or maybe it's Headmistress Larriby's and Mr. Grimeley's own little test?" Sam said as some gravy ran down his chin. Ick. "The less people they tell, the less likely we're able to find our stuff."

Logan's fingers tapped the bottom of his chin. Sam picked up on the signal and wiped the gravy from his face. Ellie and I laughed.

"But, either way, no one is saying," I looked at Ellie, "or thinking, a thing."

We sat in silence, contemplating what we could do next.

"What if we break into Old Lady Larriby's office? Maybe she has something in there that can point us in the right direction," Sam offered enthusiastically. Really, having Ellie read her teachers' minds didn't get us too far, so this was probably the next best thing.

"Yeah," Logan added, "if Headmistress Larriby and Mr. Grimeley are the only two who know where our stuff is hidden, then chances are we can find something in there."

"Especially if she needs to lock it up like that. Something big has to be in there!" exclaimed Sam.

"But if we get caught?" Ellie asked. "It is a bit risky."

"If we do it right, we won't get caught." I realized how confident I sounded. All eyes were on me—even Ellie's. I needed to come up with something fast.

"Okay … Logan, what if you use your Friday power to disappear?" I paused, hoping the rest of the plan would come to me in the next few seconds.

Three sets of eyes prompted me to go on.

"Of course we would do this after Mrs. Larriby has gone to her private room for the night and the rest of P.A. is sound asleep."

"Do you think she lives here all year round?" Ellie asked totally off-topic, twirling a few strands of flat-ironed hair around her finger. Ditzy, much?

"Back to the topic at hand," Logan stated firmly and sent a crooked smile my way.

"And then you could just sneak into the room, and find something … anything that could lead us to our stuff."

Sam opened his mouth to speak, but was cut off by Logan.

"I can do it, but I need another few days or so to build up the strength. I've used my Friday power a lot the last week, and my energy is drained."

I thought back to him disappearing on the bus, disappearing the night we snuck in the boys' room, and I'm sure he disappeared a lot during his power-intensive classes. That would get exhausting.

"It wouldn't matter," said Sam matter-of-factly, finally getting his word in.

"Why not?" I asked.

"Didn't any of you notice the giant locking keypad on the door?"

My eyes immediately shot to Sam's.

As if he read my mind, he shook his head. "I tried last year."

My jaw dropped. Sam really was a total rebel.

He continued. "My Wednesday powers didn't work with it. We would need the actual combination."

The breaking in idea came to a dead-end quick.

"We have our meetings with nostril-man Mr. Grimeley,

so why don't I try reading him?" Ellie said, trying to redeem herself from today's nose-picking discovery of Mr. Brotwurst's that was pretty much worthless to our cause.

"Maybe we could try to find out some info again, and then we can give the whole breaking in thing a shot," Logan said, nodding his head as two pieces of hair fell in his face. Yet again.

Part of me wanted to reach over there and push them out of the way, but instead I concentrated really hard on moving them away using my Monday power. What harm could that do? Plus, we all agreed that we needed to practice as much as possible.

As I concentrated on the hair, in the corner of my eye I caught Logan's wrist tracing the spoon around the edge of his plate, attempting to get every last bit of make-me-wanna-barf food that was stuck to it. Just as the strands were about to move from his face, the whole gross food-on-spoon thought popped into my head, and before I could make it stop, stuffing and gravy projected from the spoon. Most of the grossness landed on the floor, but a few chunks splattered on Ellie's perfect little pink cardigan.

"Eeeek! Poppy! What the heck?" Ellie bolted up, scooped the stuffing off her cardigan, and threw it, ick, back at me.

"I didn't mean to. I swear," I said brushing the glob from my tank top and onto the table.

She spun around so fast that strawberries flew off her tray and into my hair. "Let's just find our stupid stuff and get the heck out of here. I can't deal with the ugliness that is *you* anymore." The look she gave me as she walked out the door told me that she truly could not stand the sight of me.

I picked the strawberry pieces out of my hair, and looked across the table to see the boys uproariously laughing.

"Meow," Logan said, with fingers bent out like a cat.

They may have been amused, but I wasn't.

Chapter Fourteen

*B*FF *Veronica,*

I totally can't believe I'm actually handwriting you a letter. I mean, yes we write out our notes to each other in school and stuff, but a hand-written letter? Anyway, it's been only a couple of days here, and guess what? My powers are getting better. Really … they are! Although they probably aren't as awesome as they should be, I was able to write with chalk in my Power Academy class. No Hands! We are going to start working on moving heavier stuff soon. Miss Maggie says that she's impressed by me! Yippee!

So, you'll never guess what??? There is a chance that I will be coming home early! I could even be home before you get this through old snail mail. Okay, so this place is a total nightmare, and that's mainly cause of Headmistress Larriby, greasy-nostril-man Mr. Grimeley, and the fact that they totally took Pickle hostage and are hiding her—I will explain that whole disaster at a later time. Craziness. Not to mention the worst part of camp—fakeity-fake-o Ellie Preston who is nice to me one minute, but terrible the next. I tried Mondaying it up yesterday, and it kind of backfired. Some stuffing and gravy kind of stuck in her hair, and so she hasn't talked to me since. Ugh. BTW, she's my roommate. I feel like the last two years of her nastiness are on repeat. Over and over again, and I can't get away because she's always HERE! She makes snide remarks under her breath and blatantly ignores me. So annoying.

I miss you bunches, and can't wait to spend the rest of the summer hanging out. Just cross your fingers that my powers will work well enough to let me get out of here early!

Xoxo,

Poppy

"Fakeity-fake-o Ellie?" I heard Ellie's shrill voice come from behind me. She plopped a bottle of nail polish down on the dresser. This girl was seriously painting her nails every single day.

I guess her whole silent treatment was up. I tried apologizing like fifty times yesterday and at least ten more times just this morning, and instead of even glancing up at me, she would simply go back to filing her nails. She really was obsessed with them.

"Could you at least attempt to stay out of my thoughts?" I said, rolling my eyes. "That's what got you here in the first place." Two can play the snotty game. And I was tired of trying to win her over with kindness.

"And if I knew I'd be stuck with *you* then I definitely wouldn't have used them back at Nova Elementary." Her eyes burned into mine as she angrily pulled her hair back in a messy bun.

I could never get the messy bun thing to look right on me.

She threw herself on her bed and sighed heavily.

I did the same. There was that strange awkward silence again.

I sighed. She sighed. We lay there across from each other just ... well ... sighing. It was like each of us had something to say, but were too afraid to say it.

This girl was impossible!

As if we both read each other's thoughts, we sat up at exactly the same time.

"It's just ..." we said simultaneously.

"You go," Ellie demanded.

"No, you go."

She sat across from me cross-legged with her eyes cast down to her fluorescent-pink yoga pants. It kind of looked like she was either going to cry or she was just concentrating on something really hard.

She finally looked up after like a trillion minutes of silence, and when she did, I thought that I could see a little bit of wetness in the corner of her right eye.

"I just feel like I have to always use my powers because—" Whatever she was about to say must be pretty darn good, but it also made me feel uncomfortable. Her eyes darted back down toward her pants. "Because I don't know how to get by without reading minds." Her eyes met mine for a second, and then looked back down at the carpet below. Ellie was insecure. She looked me directly in the eyes. "And the—"

"But you get by just fine," I cut her off, trying to hold back the bitterness, thinking about how she always seemed to "get by" by being a witch and especially nasty to me. My voice softened. "Just think how lucky you are that you can use your Thursday power whenever you want, Ellie." She really was lucky. "All I want is to be able to control mine, but every time I think I have it all under control, everything goes crazy. Like last night at dinner for example."

She let out a chuckle, which was hard to believe considering her angry reaction to one of my truly accidental Monday disasters. She laughed some more and her head fell forward so that a few strands of hair escaped from her bun and covered her face. "Or the chair incident with Headmistress Larriby."

I caved and joined in with her laughing, thinking about Larriby's body plopping to the ground. "Yeah. That chair thing was pretty epi—"

"What did you just say?" she said abruptly, tucking the pieces of hair from her face and into the hair tie. Her big brown eyes locked with mine, her mouth hanging wide open.

She was sitting two feet away from me, how did she not hear it? I spoke louder and slower this time. "I said that the whole chair thing *was* pretty epic."

"Why would you say that?" Ellie demanded.

Okay. This was confusing. "Because you just mentioned it. Du-uh."

Ellie's eyes grew even bigger, and then she cautiously spoke. "I never said anything about the chair incident," she said with a gulp, "out loud."

"What do you mean? I heard you, Ellie."

She just stared at me. "I never said anything about it at all, Poppy," she emphasized.

Obviously the nail polish fumes were getting to her head. "Um, you're not making any sense at all. I heard you say it, Ellie."

We stared at each other for a moment until Ellie broke the awkward silence.

"Well, whatever. I'm sure it was just some fluke," she said casually, flicking her wrist as she spoke, like shooing away a fly.

Her eyes darted to the clock, and mine followed. Yuck. We had our check-in with Grimeley in a few minutes. I pushed what just might or might not have happened out of my mind. We had a plan in place for this meeting, and I needed to focus on that.

"Now tell me about the progress you've been making." Mr. Grimeley said in his squeaky voice. A pen hovered over a notebook that sat on his baggy pants. I stared at the center of his face, pretty sure that his nostrils had gotten even bigger over the last few days. If we looked hard enough, maybe we would find our stuff hidden up there.

Ellie made snorting noises in an attempt to hold back a laugh. I was pretty sure she had read that thought right out of my head.

"Mr. Prince, you go first," Mr. Grimeley sneered.

Logan looked at me, winked, and then began. "It's going a lot better than that first day. I disappeared on command in my power intensive class today." He stopped there, not wanting to give away too much information … just like we had all agreed.

Nostril-man Grimeley wriggled in his seat a little and then scribbled down some notes.

"Are you writing this stuff down to report back to Mrs. Larriby?" Sam asked, taking him off guard.

"I … oh … don't know what you're talking about," Mr. Grimeley said totally unconvincingly while giggling erratically. Such an odd man. "Of course not. No. The answer is no. Nope," he babbled and then ended the babbling with a loud snort.

Strange little man.

He quickly changed the subject. "And what about you, Miss Mayberry?"

I was getting so tired of all these adults calling us by our last names. Seriously, my parents named me Poppy for a reason. Just use Poppy for goodness's sake.

"Well. Not so well," I said, much more convincingly than Mr. Grimeley's lie.

Logan, Sam, and Ellie frowned in (fake) concern.

"Miss Maggie asked us to paint a smiley face on a canvas today in order to practice control."

Mr. Grimeley wrote down everything I said, word for word, surely to report back to Mrs. Larriby later. "Continue, Miss Mayberry," he pushed.

Ugh. It's Poppy.

"And just when I had the brush touching the canvas, it flew across the room and hit Matilda right on the behind. Her butt was totally sky blue. She looked like a smurf!"

Everyone in the teeny office giggled. Minus Mr.

Grimeley. His pen vigorously wrote on the paper. But behind that stoic appearance, there was a tiniest hint of a smirk. He loved thinking my powers were not coming along at all. Nice.

Okay, so maybe I was purposefully mixing up my facts a little. My brush did, in fact, fly to the ground, but I used my powers to get it back up. Tara's (one of the three "T" sisters) brush was the one that actually hit Matilda in the butt.

Sam stared directly into Mr. Grimeley's eyes. He moved his index finger up and down, and up and down. Each time it went up, the lamplight on Mr. Grimeley's desk went out. Each time his finger went down, the light came back on. He was totally toying with him, and I loved every second of it.

"And I am *really* struggling with mine," Sam boasted while continuing the flicking of the lights on and off.

In one swift movement, the lamp's cord tore out of the wall outlet and hit the side of the desk with a loud *SNAP*. We all jumped at the sound.

Mr. Grimeley was a Monday. Enough said.

"I see you are doing quite well then," he said to Sam through a grimace and turned his head. "And what about you, Miss Preston?"

"Her name is Ellie," I said, annoyed with the last-name thing now.

Ellie actually smiled at me. "I just can't stop listening to people's thoughts," she said, batting her eyelashes.

Mr. Grimeley shifted uncomfortably in his seat once again.

She concentrated on Mr. Grimeley and then crinkled her nose. "I mean, you, for instance, Mr. Grimeley, are thinking about a tuna fish and mushroom sandwich, which is totally gross, and quite possibly not what you really want to think about." She exaggerated the word *really*, and that made Grimeley wince. A few pieces of gray hair stuck to his sweaty forehead. Logan noticed them too.

He's nervous, Logan mouthed to me.

I nodded and smiled. It was working.

"So where exactly are you and Mrs. Larriby hiding Pickle?" I asked, taking the anxiety-ridden, sweaty Grimeley off-guard. Our goal was to get him flustered, and then hopefully he would let his guard down. That way, maybe Ellie could read something.

"Well … well, I'm not really sure where … uhrm …" he stuttered.

Mr. Grimeley quickly gathered his notes and literally pushed Ellie toward the library door. "Meeting is over for today," he said.

Before Ellie was completely out of sight I caught a wink from her eye. That was the signal that she was able to get something.

Our once-dreaded meeting with Mr. Grimeley might have actually been a success.

We sat around the dinner table cracking up.

"And did you see the sweat dripping from his pen? So nervous. Priceless. And I bet Old Lady Larriby is tearing him apart right now!" Logan said between laughing and chewing on a bite of macaroni and cheese.

Favorite. Food. Ever. And so much better than leftover stuffing grossness. Seriously, that stuff was the epitome of disgusting cafeteria food.

"When do you think Ellie's gonna get here?" Sam asked excitedly. It was official, in the short time Sam had known Ellie, he was totally crushing on her. Logan's knowing grin told me that he sensed it too.

I looked up at the clock to see that dinner started like fifteen minutes ago, and got a little nervous myself. "She said earlier that she wanted to change her shirt after our meeting."

"Into another pink one?" Logan asked.

I liked how funny he was.

"So, you two are on speaking terms now?" Logan asked, cocking his head to the side so that a few hairs fell over his eyes. There was no way I was going to attempt to move them with my Monday power again.

"Yeah, I guess so." I shrugged it off.

"Awww … you're besties now!" Sam mocked.

"Ha. Ha. Haahhh, guys. Sooooo funny," Ellie said, plunking down into the seat next to me and rolling her eyes. "Not even close to besties," she spat.

Ouch.

"Where the heck were you?" Sam asked, pushing his glasses up his nose. He really needed to look into adjusting those nose pads.

"Oh, you know … just doing a little more detective work." She smiled. It was obvious that she enjoyed calling herself a detective.

"So, I totally had every intention of going up to change," Ellie said, looking down at her perfectly fine shirt, the same one she was wearing in our meeting from earlier. She set her purse down on the table, reached one hand in, looked around the cafeteria, and then pulled something out. We all scrunched in closer to shield the piece of folded paper she held in her hand we knew must be important.

"What is it?" Sam asked.

Ellie leaned in closer. "As greasy Grimeley practically threw me out of the library, I could totally get into his head." She cleared her throat and pushed her bangs to the side. "Is that any good?" she asked, pointing at the plate full of macaroni in front of Sam.

"Ellie! Get to the point," Logan barked.

"Yeah. So, he kept muttering stuff over and over in his head …" She paused. "I thought in his head, at least."

She grinned like she was proud of this fact.

"And what did you hear?" Logan pressed, pushing the macaroni out of the way.

"Well …" Ellie was excited because she began twirling a few strands of hair around her fingers and her eyes got super big. "He was crossing the main foyer hallway from the library toward Mrs. Larriby's office. I tiptoed, like, totally quiet."

I glanced down at her clacking kitten heels and found that hard to believe.

"I was quiet enough, Poppy," she said, rolling her eyes.

"So, did you read his mind or not?"

She continued, ignoring my question. And here I thought we were starting to patch things up.

"As I got closer to him, I heard him muttering some stuff under his breath. Like, out loud."

"Told you he's strange," Sam said, looking around at us all. His eyes lingered a little longer on Ellie's. She smiled back at him.

"Did you read his mind or not?" I asked again.

She beamed, looking at me. "You'd be proud, Poppy. I didn't have to."

We leaned in even closer. The rim on Sam's cowboy hat hit my head, so I backed away a few inches.

"I think he was making himself think nonsensical stuff, like earlier with the mushrooms and tuna fish, so he wouldn't give anything away. So his thoughts were worthless, but what came out of his mouth totally mattered."

Ellie had a way of making a story last a really long time. My eyes urged her to continue. The blank stares from Sam and Logan told me that they were ready for her to get to the point too.

"Anyway, I think he was so focused on not thinking anything, he was literally saying out loud over and over again what he really needed to remember."

"So, basically he was thinking out loud," Logan restated quickly, again prompting her to get to the point.

We all stared down at Ellie's hand with the folded up piece of paper like it contained some ancient treasure. She ran her fingers over the edges.

"And that's it, what he was saying? Written down?" Logan asks pointing to it.

"Yep." She smiled broadly and gently unfolded the paper. "This is what I heard him say."

7-7-6-0

We stared at Ellie with puzzled expressions.

"Um … okay. And what does it mean?" Sam asked the question we were all thinking.

"Well, then I watched him go to Headmistress Larriby's office door with that giant light-up keypad thingy, and I would bet that is the number that he punched to get in there," she said sing-songy while her manicured finger pointed to the scribbled numbers.

"Sweet," Sam said. He reached his hand up and gave Ellie a high five.

"And I didn't even have to use my powers," she said, flicking her hair behind her back and pushing her chest out proud as a peacock.

"In the meantime though, let's try to find out as much as possible. We don't know for sure her office will have any info," offered Logan.

That never occurred to me. Maybe our hope of finding something in her office was useless. But at least we had somewhere to start.

I turned to Ellie. "Today you were a real detective," I said, smiling. "No powers needed." Then I look directly at Logan and Sam. "The rest might be up to us. We just need to figure out if those numbers will get us into her office and if there is actually anything of value in there."

"To keep it locked up with a freakin' lock like that, she has to be hiding something pretty darn important," Logan said, looking me straight in the eye. Then he added confidently, "And we're going to find out what it is."

Chapter Fifteen

The next morning flew by without any of us having the chance to check out Headmistress Larriby's office. Sure, we all knew what the passkey combination was, but there was rarely a time when the office was left unattended. Grimeley or Larriby were always there. The fact that when they entered the room they allowed the door to open just enough to slip their bodies in, (for Larriby, that meant the door was open pretty wide) made it even more apparent that there was something in there they didn't want us to see. But that gave us even more of a reason to break in.

Since it hadn't happened yet, we all vowed that we needed to get in there within the next few days. At this point, Pickle had been held who-knows-where for what seemed like forever. This needed to end. And it needed to end soon! The four of us decided that the beginning of the end would be tonight. All we had to do was stay out of trouble until then. And for the boys, that may have been more difficult than I thought.

"Mr. Bricker and Mr. Priiiice?" Blind-as-a-bat Mrs. Barkdoll wailed in Nova History class for like the quadtrillionth time, calling out attendance. Logan corrected her twice yesterday on the whole last-name thing.

"It's Prince, you know, with an 'n,'" he had said, and we both giggled together.

But it seemed that Mrs. Barkdoll may have been just as hearing-impaired as she was vision-impaired because she still couldn't get it right. You'd think she would get it after a few days of being at Power Academy.

"Mr. Bricker and Mr. Priiiice?" she bellowed again, still getting his name wrong. "Tsk. Tsk," she said wiggling her pen toward … well … no one really. "Do students not realize the punishment for tardiness to my class?" She walked down the next row, checking off students as she went.

Mrs. Barkdoll told us on the first day that if we were late to her class that it would result in an evening of "close-monitoring." Basically, that meant that greasy Grimeley or clothes-too-tight Larriby would be babysitting whomever for the evening. For obvious reasons, that could not happen. Without all four of us together tonight, there was no way we even had a chance of breaking in. We needed the guys. It was all or nothing.

I thought back to the first day in History of Nova class. "No more than five minutes late, hear me," Mrs. Barkdoll had said then. And I could tell she meant it.

I glanced at the clock. It was nine-twenty. The class began at nine-fifteen. My palms started to sweat, and I noticed Ellie's pink flats tapping harder than usual on the floor below. This was not good. Not good at all. If Sam and Logan didn't show up within the next five seconds, then we definitely wouldn't be able to get our stuff back and would have to stay … gulp … here.

My eyes were glued to the clock. *Tick. Tick. Tick.* Just a few more seconds to go. *Tick.* 9:21 a.m. It was official, they were late.

Ellie sighed at the same time as me, as if she read my mind. Well, she probably did.

Mrs. Barkdoll got back to the front of the room and read off their names one more time.

"Mr. Bricker and Mr.—"

"Prince?" a voice bellowed from the back of the room. I spun around and smiled. It was Logan.

"I ... uh ..." Mrs. Barkdoll stumbled on her words. She gathered herself. "Um ... where did you come from, young man?"

"Oh, I was here the whole time, but didn't realize you were calling my name," he said, shooting a wink in my direction. There was no way Mrs. Barkdoll noticed his small eye movement.

"Then why did you not speak up earlier?" She pursed her lips in frustration.

All eyes were on Logan. "I was just so engrossed in chapter twelve, reading about Tuesdays' teleporting powers, I simply couldn't concentrate on *anything* else," he said so convincingly, even I almost believed him. "I would do anything to be a Tuesday." He sighed.

Obviously, blind-as-a-bat Barkdoll was swayed. "Do you know that I'm a Tuesday?" she asked, grinning from ear to ear.

Of course, we all knew. She had only told us about thirty times.

"I didn't!" he exaggerated, even more convincingly than before. "I just think it would be wonderful to be able to teleport."

Mrs. Barkdoll disappeared and then instantly reappeared next to Logan. "It is rather fun," she said, nudging his shoulder. Logan was good. He was really good.

She shoved the seating chart back up to her face and then squinted toward the clock. I followed her gaze. 9:23 a.m. I sighed. Sam was really late.

"Now, where is that Mr. Bri—"

BOOM! The door slammed behind heavy-breathing, hat-wearing Sam.

"Mr. Bricker, you are late for my class, and you know what that—"

"Whatever do you mean?" he interrupted, doing an Ellie-like eyelash batting. Sam was almost as convincing as Logan.

Ellie frowned. She knew just as I did—he was caught red-handed.

Mrs. Barkdoll continued, "Well, you are over five minutes late, and you know my rule—"

"But I'm not," he stated matter-of-factly, pointing to the clock above the front board. I watched the minute hand fly back three little black lines.

Mrs. Barkdoll's white sneakers squeaked with each step she took until she was directly underneath of it. "Hmmm. I swore it wa—" She cleared her throat. "It seems I was wrong," she admitted, and brushed it off, chuckling, "maybe it's time for some new glasses."

The rest of the class laughed. I was sure Mrs. Barkdoll thought they were giggling with her, but they all knew just as much as I did what Sam had done. He was definitely good. I looked at the clock. 9:20 a.m. on the nose. He was an awesome power-manipulating Wednesday. That was a close one.

But why were those boys late anyway?

After that nerve-wracking History of Nova class, I walked into Miss Maggie's room to be greeted by her fun (and did I mention, awesome?) accent.

"Welcome, dearest Poppy," she said with what I swore was a twinkle in her eye.

After we all sat down Miss Maggie sauntered over to the bookshelf in the corner of the room. "I have a surprise for you all today," she said, glancing in my direction. She daintily lifted her right hand and pointed her finger toward the wall. In a quick flick of the wrist the bookcase made a rumbling sound as it glided to the right, revealing a built-in set of six shelves.

"Wow!" Matilda shouted and clapped her hands. "Too cool."

Miss Maggie's heels clicked as she paced in front of the shelf and began. "Before this was Power Academy, they used to do experiments on Weekdays in the hopes of better understanding our powers." All eyes were glued on her. That sounded creepy. "There are secret compartments like this all over campus," she said nonchalantly, as if explaining to us something as ordinary as tying a shoe.

But that wasn't ordinary. Thinking of those disturbing old haunted hospital and insane asylum movies my dad likes to watch, a shiver went down my spine at the mention of the words *old* and *experiments*. Ick.

"Back then, the doctors liked to keep some of the medications and medical tools hidden away from the crazed patients," she said with her voice hushed in a way that made it sound like she was telling some sort of ghost story. I felt like we should have all been sitting around a campfire.

I looked over to see everyone staring at her, wide-eyed. I could feel my own eyes bulging out of their sockets. This place was just too much and too creepy.

The hidden compartment that she was pointing to was not filled with medical tools and medicine like the ones years ago. Instead, boxes of candy, chocolate-covered pretzels, sweets, and gummy bears lined the shelves. Stocked by Miss Maggie.

Miss Maggie flicked her wrist once more. We all gasped as the bookcase slid shut over the shelves.

"It's that easy," she said, snapping her finger.

"Maybe for her," I muttered so that Matilda could hear me.

"Move the bookcase back using your powers alone, no hands, and you all get what's inside of it," Miss Maggie said, smiling.

Awesome! Those were some high stakes. Overall, Power Academy was lacking in the "bad foods" department and some sugary goodness would be fantabulous!

Miss Maggie read off our names in the order of our turn. I was dead last on the list.

Each of the six other Mondays took their turn. They were pretty unsuccessful. The closest person to even moving the shelf was Matilda. The shelf wiggled and wobbled a little bit, but that was about it. Poor girl.

But Matilda remained upbeat as usual. "Next time I'll get it." I loved that girl's optimism, and wondered if I would be seeing her around Nova Middle next year. I hoped so. Through the few short interactions we've had at Power Academy, I decided that we could totally be friends.

"And now you, Poppy. You're everyone's only hope for candy," Miss Maggie dramatically stated, throwing the back of her hand to her head.

"Goooooo, Poppy," Matilda said like an overenthusiastic cheerleader. I imagined pom-poms shaking in each of her hands.

This was definitely the heaviest and bulkiest thing I had ever tried to move with my Monday power yet. Well, this was the heaviest and bulkiest thing I'd ever had to move in general, really. Monday power or not.

Miss Maggie's British voice cheered me on even more. "I know it's asking a lot of you, Poppy. But I am confident that if you concentrate hard enough, you can do it."

I stared at that case full of books covering the case full of treats and slowly raised my hand like I had watched Miss Maggie do many times before.

"Pointing at the object helps your control," she had said the other week during the whole painting exercise. The one that each of us failed at. Bummer.

I pointed my index finger at the shelf. *Slide over, slide over, slide over*, I willed it.

The shelf leaned slightly to the right.

"Okay, just a little bit more," Miss Maggie said. "Nice and slow."

"Come on, Poppy!"

"You got this!"

"Just concentrate."

All the encouragement distracted me for a moment, and then I used it as inspiration to push myself even further.

A loud screeching sound came from the case as it began moving even more slightly to the right. Awesome! It was about two inches from where it was when I began. That was a start at least, right?

"Keep it going, Poppy!"

My index finger was steady, pointing at the shelf. The rest of my fingers were digging so hard into my palm that I was sure there would be finger indentations on it when all was said and done.

"You go, girl," Matilda cheered.

"Pahhh-ppy, Pahhh-ppy, Pahhh-ppy," everyone chanted. I was sure they were more excited at the prospect of candy more than anything else.

I could do this. Only two feet to go, and I was in the clear.

"Pahhh-ppy, Pahhh-ppy, Pahhh-p—"

And that's when it went wrong. Instead of sliding the rest of the way, the shelf leaned over so that all of its weight rested on the bottom right corner. I began to panic, afraid that it might crash on its side.

Set back down, gently, I willed it. But instead of setting down gently, the shelf rocked back down on its left bottom corner and then swayed back and forth a few times. The books slid from one side to the other with each rock, and then they landed in a position that made it look like an earthquake had just hit Power Academy.

When the shelf finally came to a rest, it had completely covered the hidden compartment—looking exactly as it did before we even began.

Fail.

"Awwww." Matilda sighed. I felt her hand on my shoulder. "You're bound to get it soon. You are so close. Just so close, Poppy."

Although I was not as advanced as the Mondays back in Nova, I felt pretty good compared to the others here. I mean, at least I got the entire shelf to move, right? Not that the others here weren't good, they just needed some time. And I could tell that they all would make amazing Mondays by the end of the summer.

The fact that I didn't complete Miss Maggie's big lesson for multiple days in a row totally made me nervous. Especially since we had to find Pickle and all the other stuff, and I hadn't even proven my Monday power yet. I thought about my poor furry girl.

Before I could even say thanks for the other students' encouragements, the bell rang and everyone gathered their stuff for lunch.

"See ya tomorrow, Poppy," Matilda said, smiling at me. If we had any luck tonight, then maybe I wouldn't.

As I headed toward the door, I felt something hit my back. I spun around to see that everyone had left the classroom except for Miss Maggie who was working on something behind her desk. After taking a second look around the room, I glanced at the floor to see a perfectly folded paper airplane crashed next to my feet.

I unfolded the wings to see the words *Embrace your powers. Good Luck, Poppy.*

Miss Maggie looked up and winked. I tilted my head to the side and hesitantly smiled back.

I read back over the message a few times as I walked to lunch and shoved it into the back pocket of my jean skirt. Did Miss Maggie know about the challenge? I was totally confused.

And then it dawned on me that she might have created that last lesson specifically for me. But why?

Chapter Sixteen

At lunch, Logan and Sam filled us in on why they were so late to blind-as-a-bat Barkdoll's class this morning and almost jeopardized our secret break-in we had planned for tonight.

"So, we decided to leave a bit early for class in hopes of seeing if we can use those numbers Ellie found us," Sam said with a goofy grin aimed at Ellie.

"And, did you get in?" I perked up. Maybe this was the break we needed.

"It didn't happen," said Logan. "Of course, Larriby was in there."

Ellie and I frowned at each other.

"But, we overheard parts of a conversation between Mrs. Larriby and someone else—"

"Who was it? Who was the other person?" Ellie interrupted, eager as ever.

Sam jumped in, "We couldn't really see, 'cause that person sat right behind her office door."

"But it was definitely a woman, we know that much."

Logan and Sam shrugged in unison.

"But the weird thing—"

"Yeah?" Ellie interrupted again.

I smirked at Logan, and we shook our heads. Typical Ellie.

"Headmistress Larriby didn't even sound like Larriby at all," added Sam.

"What do you mean?" I asked, knowing that there was no mistaking her manly voice, like, ever.

"She was all nervous-sounding and stuff and stuttering all over the place." Logan smirked. "Whoever Larriby was talking to made her really jumpy."

I laughed at the thought of something or someone actually intimidating Headmistress Larriby. "I would love to have heard that." But what did this have to do with anything?

Ellie's eyes darted from mine and then across the table to the boys. "Okay, but what does this have to do with anything?" she asked, reading me. I tilted my head in annoyance, and then just let it go. Ellie was just being typical Ellie, and I realized that I would never be able to change that.

She smirked.

"The other woman in there made it very clear that she was not happy with Headmistress Larriby and how 'everything' was going," Logan said, and his eyes glanced sideways at Sam.

"What do you mean, 'everything'?" I asked.

Sam jumped in again. "From what we heard, we think—" He hesitated. "Well, we *know* that their conversation had something to do with," he looked around the crowded cafeteria to see if anyone was looking and whispered, "*the challenge* she gave to us." He and Logan exchanged glances, like they were unsure if they wanted to say more.

"Go on, *puh-lease*," Ellie said impatiently.

"How do you *know* it has to do with us, though?" I jumped in before Ellie read it and said it.

"The woman mentioned something about maybe Mrs. Larriby had 'chosen unwisely' again," said Sam with those air-quote thingies.

"Wait … what? I mean, chosen unwisely could be about a lot of things, and if we don't even know who was in there with her, then how could you know it even relates to us?"

The boys hesitated again. They were hiding something. I could tell.

"Just spit it out," Ellie spat and grimaced at Logan. "Don't worry about hurting our feelings. We can take it," she said totally unconvincingly, noticeably reading his mind.

The boys looked at each other and then sighed together.

"This person said to Larriby that if the chosen four really have *potential* then they should be able to complete the challenge within the next day or two."

"That's how we know the conversation was about us," Sam said, pushing his glasses up his nose.

I thought back to totally bombing at Miss Maggie's challenge just thirty minutes ago. Only two days to show that I had mastered my power? Craziness!

"There's more, I know it," said Ellie.

The boys said nothing.

"Come on, guys. Tell me … uhr … us," she demanded.

"Fine." Logan's green eyes met mine and softened. "Then this person said that it was probably …" He paused.

"Probably what?" Ellie demanded, becoming flustered.

Logan spoke cautiously. "That it was probably the girls holding the four back. We heard her say that the two girls would be the reason Team Five would fail." Once Logan finished he flinched away, waiting for Ellie's backlash.

Sam put his hands up in surrender. "Told you it was about us." He paused. "Please, don't shoot the messengers." He shyly linked eyes with Ellie and faked a smile.

I played Logan's words over in my head, attempting to understand.

One: We only had a few days to work together, find our

stuff, and prove our powers were strong enough to get the heck out of here. And I was waaayyyy behind.

Two: Ellie and I were the reason we might not get to leave early.

Who was that woman?

Surprisingly, Ellie didn't say a thing right away, but I could tell that her anger, or hurt, or whatever it was, was brewing. The reddening of her face told me she was not happy, and would burst at any second. Unfortunately, I was right.

"What the heck? This is totally ridiculous! How can that … that … woman, whoever she is, say such a preposterous thing? I am A-MAAAY-ZING with my powers, and everyone knows that and knows that I shouldn't be here anyway. YOU, maybe," she yelled, pointing down at me and pushing herself up from the table, and then continued, "but definitely not me!"

I stood and hesitantly placed my right hand on Ellie's shoulder, unsure if she would snap at me or not. Even though the words she spoke had stung, I had to calm her down before she made an even bigger scene. After all, Headmistress Larriby had said that if anyone else knew about our challenge, then we would be stuck here for sure.

"Look. We know you're great, Ellie. It's just—"

Ellie flicked my hand away, "Don't even try, Poppy! I still blame you for me even being here in the first place!"

As she turned to stomp off, I was pretty sure I noticed tears welling in the corners of her eyes.

Drama Queen, Logan mouthed.

"We'll talk later, guys," I said, following after Ellie. It was Ellie and I who needed to talk now.

I stood outside of our room, listening and waiting for her sobs to die down. Ellie sounded awful. It was obvious that she had issues with me, and I knew I had to find out exactly what those issues were.

It was now or never.

I placed my knuckles to the door and knocked three times. No answer.

I knocked again. "Ellie, I know you're in there," I said with force.

No answer.

"Look, if we want to get out of here, we need to at least talk to one another," I said gingerly, hoping she would say something. She could at least give me one of her annoyed sighs. Anything.

No answer.

"Please, Ellie." I leaned against the door. Her sobs had died down, and I knew she was listening.

Why do you hate me? I thought, knowing she was listening in.

And then the door clicked open. It was noon, and Ellie was standing in the doorway in her pink pajamas. Although the tears had dried, her cheeks puffed up from her crying.

I hesitated, unsure if she would snap at me again.

"I'm not mad anymore, promise," Ellie said softly.

I entered the room and sat down on my lopsided bed across from her.

"I don't hate you, Poppy—"

"Well, you sure act like it," I cut her off. My words came out harsher than I intended. But I knew they were true and that I meant them.

"I deserve that," she said. "You shouldn't be nice to me at all after the way I've treated you."

"Is it 'cause of the whole headband incident last year?" I asked, looking for her reaction.

She shrugged and flicked her wrist. "I've forgotten about that," she said convincingly, as if she truly did forget about that.

I thought back to the nasty looks, hurtful notes, and the mean tricks since then. "I thought the headband thingy was the reason you've been so mean to me, though." But deep down, I knew her hatred of me started way before that.

She uncrossed her legs and moved to the edge of the bed. "I guess it's just …" She sighed. Her legs swung nervously back and forth. "That headband thing was just another excuse."

I didn't want to cut her off this time. I was hopeful that we might actually finish the conversation we began a few days ago. I said nothing and thought nothing, wanting her to go on without my prompting in any way.

She did. "It was a reason to be mean to you," she said quickly, looking away. But I could tell that she was trying to hold back tears. "I hate the fact that you are naturally smart and good at stuff. You don't have to manipulate people through *your* powers like I do."

Was it possible that Ellie was actually jealous of me?

"Honestly, I didn't even know what manipulate meant until I looked it up after Mr. Wobble-Wible used it that day in his office when we got sent here," Ellie said.

I could believe that.

"But *you* would know what it means," she continued, her eyes still avoiding mine. "I would totally fail my classes if I didn't use my Thursday powers. I just can't remember things, and it's easier just listening to the answers and stuff." She finally made eye contact with me. "I'm not naturally smart like you are, Poppy."

Was perfect pretty girl Ellie Preston saying that she's not really that perfect? Other than the snoring and the gross retainer, this was the most human and honest I had ever seen her.

"You need to give yourself more credit," I said, actually feeling sorry for her. "I bet you would do just fine without the whole mind-reading thing. You don't need it to feel better about yourself." I realized that came out a bit too adult-sounding. "I mean, you're smart in your own way."

She nodded. "Maybe." She paused, and I could tell she was conflicted and fighting with herself over something. "You wanna know something crazy?"

I nodded.

"Something I've never told anyone." Her face was super serious now. "And I probably shouldn't tell you of all people," her voice trailed off.

"Sure," I smiled. Oh my gosh. Ellie was going to confide in me? This sure was a strange day. Heck, the last week had been strange.

"Remember when we used to hang out when we were like, really little?"

I nodded. Of course I remembered it. We grew up, and still lived just a few houses from one another. The Prestons' home was three times the size of mine and had a five-foot tall stone wall surrounding it, which made it look totally out of place in our middle-class neighborhood. Nevertheless, when we were small Ellie's mom would always have me over for soda and snacks and stuff. Ellie and I would go swimming, play with dolls, and set up fun lemonade stands. Once, we even put together a neighborhood fun fair with swings and corndogs and everything. That's when Ellie was nice and we were friends, not best friends, but friends at least, and before ...

Ellie's voice broke in. "My Mom wanted me to be a Monday like her so badly," she said, reaching for the tissue tucked into her pajama pocket.

"Really?" I asked, not knowing what else to say, and forgetting for a moment that Ellie's mother was a Monday just like me.

"Yeah, and she never realized that I noticed the way she would look at you, Poppy—even if your powers weren't in yet."

I was in too much shock to respond.

"Almost like, she wanted you as a daughter, a Monday just like her, and not me. A stupid mind-reading Thursday."

I watched two tears trickle down Ellie's cheek. That's when I realized that all those years of vicious looks, nasty remarks, and all-around cruelty were because Ellie was jealous of ME. Not because I was a loser, or not as rich as her, or anything like that. It was out of jealousy. How could a mother make her daughter feel that way?

Ellie's face brightened a bit as she spoke. "Did you

know that moms in Nova will, like, go out of their way to have a baby on a certain day of the week?"

Wow! "No," I spoke honestly. That thought never crossed my mind. My parents loved me unconditionally, I knew that. But what Ellie said did make sense. People were crazy to have weekday powers. And then I suddenly remembered something Veronica had said over a year ago. "And I've heard that some moms will demand to send their own babies back if they're born on a weekend!" she had said. Craziness!

"Yeah. I've heard my mom say stuff to my dad about me being a Thursday, too. It always made me feel like I was a failure or something," Ellie continued through sniffles. She shook her head and then whispered, "That woman telling Larriby that we are going to fail just reminded me of that." She paused. "Reminded me that I'm not quite good enough."

The enormity of this moment hit me hard. As confident as Ellie acted on the outside, she was equally insecure on the inside. I had never, and would never know what it would be like to have a parent disapprove of me. Even if I were a powerless Saturday or Sunday, I knew for a fact that it wouldn't matter to my parents. "I know that she loves you, Ellie, no matter what weekday you are," I said, hoping to cheer her up, and took a seat on the bed next to her. "Just think of those poor Saturdays and Sundays who don't have any powers at all—those are the ones to feel sorry for. But they get by."

She nodded.

I continued. "Not to mention the rest of the world outside of Nova. They get by just fine."

She chuckled. "I guess you're right."

"I mean, the mayor's own son gets by through nose-picking," I said, hoping to cheer her up.

It worked. We laughed together.

"You're so nice, Poppy. Even after all I've done to you. Here you are, being so nice to me."

Her lower lip quivered a little. She looked away and then back at me again. I knew what she wanted to say next. "I'm just really …" her tears began to fall harder. She turned toward me. Through sobs she made out, "Sorry. I'm so sorry, Poppy." And before I knew what was happening, her two skinny arms were wrapped around me. I watched as a few of her tears dropped onto my silver flats.

Was this really happening? I had waited for the longest time for Ellie to apologize to me for all of the hurtful things she had done. But, it didn't feel as good as I had hoped. Ellie was hurt, and it made me feel sad.

Some wetness formed in my own eyes as I thought back to the end of third grade, the day that we went from friends to not-so-friends. I invited my two best friends in the world, Celia and Veronica, to my house for a sleepover.

I was super excited to have a night of pizza, s'mores, movies, and girl talk. None of us had even begun developing our weekday powers yet, so all the drama surrounding that was far from our minds then. Veronica and I waited and waited for Celia. But Celia never showed up that night.

It turned out that Ellie had told Celia that I didn't want to be friends with her anymore because I thought she was lame. Of course, that was a total lie. Ellie actually invited Celia over to her house for a sleepover that night. Celia went and was sucked into a friendship with Ellie ever since.

And now I knew what started it all. Ellie was jealous that I was a Monday. For some reason she felt the need to get back at me for something I couldn't even control. She stole one of my best friends. She treated me like dirt the last few years. And surprisingly enough, I wasn't angry with her anymore. In fact, I felt bad for her. Ellie. The girl who now crushed me in a bear hug.

I looked to the clock over her shoulder. 2:10 p.m. "We need to get those guys and get in that office," I said, scrunching my way out of the never-ending squeeze. "And prove to Headmistress Larriby and that other woman that we have plenty of potential and will not fail!"

Ellie wiped the final tears from her eyes, pinched her cheeks, put on some lip-gloss, and grabbed her purse. "You're right, Poppy," she said, squeezed my hand, and pulled me toward the door. "Let's go find Pickle."

"Um, Ellie," I said, pointing at her pajamas. The Ellie I know wouldn't be caught dead wearing those in public.

"Thanks, Poppy!" she said.

I laughed and tried to wrap my mind around what had just happened. I think Ellie and I could actually *be* friends.

Chapter Seventeen

I looked at the clock. Eight thirty sharp. I zipped my black hoodie up and over my orange necklace. It reminded me of my mom. Gosh, I missed her. If we were successful, I might see her sooner than later.

"Ellie, we have to get going."

Ellie threw her hand in my face to show me two bare fingernails. "I have two more to go. Be a little patient, Poppy. The boys aren't going anywhere without me ... us ... I mean." I caught the eye roll.

Unlike some charm bracelet, Pickle wasn't some inanimate object that could be replaced if never found. I needed to get to her. Sure, it had only been like a week, but those last few days must have been the worst of Pickle's furry little life. *Be there soon*, I thought, wishing that dogs could read minds too.

Ellie took her time brushing the nail polish over the last two fingernails. She might have been taking this whole mysterious detective thing a little too far. I mean, sure, the black outfits we had on were exactly what we needed to blend in and stuff, but black nail polish? Did she need to go that far?

Thump, thump, thump. Three knocks at the door startled me, and Ellie almost dropped the bottle of polish to the ground. We both threw robes over our semi-camouflage outfits.

Headmistress Larriby stood in the doorway with both hands on her bulging hip. "Awwww, another day went by, and you didn't find your silly little treasures. Too bad."

Her lips curled down into a fake pouty face.

She turned to leave, and then spun back around to us, forgetting something. "Good luck, ladies. You'll need it!" She smirked, giving us the strangest looking evil eye I had ever seen, and then she did one of those finger wiggle wave things. But her fingers looked like fat sausages fluttering in our direction.

If you forgot about the whole stealing and hiding of our stuff situation, Headmistress Larriby was actually quite comical, and not nearly as scary as people made her out to be—even when she announced to Logan, Sam, Ellie and I at dinner tonight that we had a new deadline to her challenge. Little did she know what we had in our possession. Four important numbers—thanks to Ellie and her non-mind reading power.

Mrs. Larriby shot me an irritated stare. "Lights out in five," she said. The door crashed behind her.

Ellie threw a few accessories into her black purse. She came prepared for anything.

"Now aren't you glad it took me a while to finish these?" she asked sarcastically, pushing the finished manicured hand in my face.

"Yes," I admitted. Normally, I'd cringe at the thought of being late for anything. But if we didn't answer the door when clothes-too-tight Larriby showed up, then we would have been in deep trouble. I guess being late was worth it in this case.

"You can tell that lady, like, totally hates kids, so why *wouldn't* she want us to leave early?" Ellie asked, tossing her pullover over her head.

"I think you said it. She hates kids. And I'm sure she wants to make our summers as miserable as possible."

"I guess."

"And," it suddenly dawned on me, "maybe she doesn't like the fact that someone could actually beat her at this little game of hers."

Ellie blinked at me. "What do you mean?"

Her eyes urged me to go on. At least she was actually

letting me tell her instead of simply reading my mind.

"She's checking up on us. She's nervous that we might actually win. You know," I did the best Headmistress Larriby voice I could, "not once has anyone been able to go home early, and I intend to keep it that way."

Ellie laughed. "That was a pretty good imitation."

"Oh, yeah?"

"If the whole Monday thing doesn't work out for you, you could totally do impersonations," she said, grinning.

"Ha. Ha. Ha." I said, emphasizing each *ha*.

"What are we waiting for? Let's get the guys."

The four of us huddled outside the library and discussed our strategy one more time. "So, all you have to do is disappear, punch in the combo, and then signal for us to come over," Sam said to Logan. "And then your part is done."

"Piece of cake," Logan said confidently, as usual.

It was hard for me to look at Sam without laughing. Like Ellie and her painted fingernails, he had gone all out for this whole reconnaissance mission. His precisely painted face matched his camouflage outfit. His strange hunting hobby paid off. This rebel of a redhead, glasses-wearing, clarinet-playing, deer-hunting Wednesday continued to surprise me.

Logan nodded, closed his eyes, and vanished into thin air. Just like that. He really was a good Friday, and he definitely didn't need to be here this summer. But I was glad that he was here.

"Do you think our stuff might actually be in the school?" Ellie asked.

It would be easy to hide a bracelet, soccer ball, and a clarinet. But was it even possible to keep a barking, whining dog hidden without anyone knowing? "There's no way she hid our stuff in this building," I whispered. "But there might be a clue in her office that could lead us to where it all is."

We were standing outside of the library, next to the staircase, so we had a direct view of Headmistress Larriby's office. Even though I couldn't see Logan, I could see the numbers on the outside lock light up as he pressed them. Seven lit up. Then seven again.

Thump. Thump. The sound of footsteps came from above us. Gosh. Couldn't we catch a break?

"Quick, over here," I said, pulling Ellie along. We crouched down underneath the winding staircase and listened as Mr. Grimeley shuffled through the upstairs foyer. If he noticed those lit-up numbers once he got downstairs, then he would be on to us. I could practically hear my heart beating in my chest.

My eyes looked over at the key lock. The light from the keypad was practically blinding in the darkness, and Mr. Grimeley would definitely see it once he reached the bottom.

"Sam, you have to do something with that light! Grimeley's gonna see."

We could all hear Grimeley's shuffles move down the stairs. It was only a matter of time…

"But I have to get a little closer, it's just too far to reach," he whispered.

"Just try it, Sam," Ellie said, batting her long eyelashes.

And that was enough to prompt him on. He pointed his finger toward the glaring numbers.

Our heads snapped up, hearing Grimeley's shuffles directly above us now. He would round the corner of the stairs and see the light at any second.

"Now," Ellie said.

Sam reached his arm out again, and the light flickered on and off a few times.

Grimeley was one step from the bottom.

The light flickered on and off and back on again. Uh-Oh.

And just as we watched Grimeley's pants-covered foot

reach the floor, the light clicked off. For good.

"Phew!" We all sighed at once.

"Nice work, Sam," Ellie said.

Sam poked his head out from behind the staircase. "He's crossing right in front of Larriby's office now," he whispered.

"I just hope Logan can stay invis—"

And before I could even finish my sentence Logan reappeared to my right. "That was a close one, guys," he said, and then looked at Sam. "Nice job, bud."

Mr. Grimeley's foot-shuffles got quieter and quieter until a door slammed and they were heard no more.

Sam totally saved our butts there, and Logan and his disappearing act was simply amazing. I found myself smiling at that last thought. Logan was pretty amazing all around.

But then I remembered what the boys told us about the conversation they overheard. Whoever was talking to Headmistress Larriby said that the "girls" would be the ones who ruin the whole challenge. It was obvious the guys had their powers under control—Ellie and I just needed to prove ours. Even though I had no idea what that meant.

"Let's try this again."

And just like that, Logan disappeared. This time *7-7-6-0* lit up without any interruptions.

Bzzz.

"We're in." Logan's voice echoed through the foyer.

After making sure nobody was in sight, we tiptoed across the hall and into the office.

"Quick, shut the door," Sam said to Ellie. He reached for the doorknob at the same time as she did and their hands touched. Sam totally planned that. The laugh flew out of my mouth before I could even stop it.

"Shhhh," Logan said. But I could see the smile underneath the finger over his mouth.

As if we'd been an investigating team forever, we each knew enough to take a corner of the room. Headmistress Larriby's office was just about the most organized one I had ever been in, so it didn't take long to get through everything we could get our hands on. We looked through stacks of organized paper, dozens of files, and over thirty notepads.

After what seemed like twenty hours of searching, (I looked at the clock and it really had only been about five minutes) we took a break.

"Nothing."

"This is ridiculous. There is nowhere else to look." Sam sighed in frustration. "All this focus on this stupid office and we—"

"Guys! Over here!" Logan whisper-yelled.

We rushed to his corner of the room and looked down at the manila folder he had spread out. There were four clipped stacks of paper in all, and our individual names were on the front cover of each one.

"Give it here," Ellie said, snatching at the sheet with her name attached to the top.

"Gheesh!" Logan exclaimed. "Impatient, much?"

She rolled her eyes.

I grabbed the one with my name and flipped through it. What was so important about these packets? The application to Power Academy that Wobble-Wible must have filled out was on top. Our personal item sheet was next, and then a card with personal information. My name, address, phone number, day, parents' names, parents' days, birthday, and time were on there as well. But then I noticed something strange.

"Guys! What's this all about?" I said, flipping my card around and pointing to the fluorescent yellow color highlighting my birthday.

Ellie plopped down on a jumbo chair in the corner situated in front of a familiar-looking bookcase. "Hey! Mine's highlighted too!" she exclaimed.

"And mine," said Logan.

All eyes watched as Sam flipped to his information sheet. "Yep!"

We set our information cards next to one another. "Whoa! Do you guys see it?" Ellie shouted.

"Shhh."

"Do you guys see it?" she whispered.

Of course we saw it. Even though the four of us were born on different days — we were born in the same week at exactly the same time. 11:59 p.m. "What does this all mean?" I asked.

Sam picked up his camo hat and scratched his red poof of hair. "I have no idea."

"Wait. I thought you were older than us?" Logan asked, flicking the hat out of Sam's hand.

Typical boys.

Sam used the back of his hand to push up his glasses. "I skipped a grade," he said nonchalantly, like it was something everyone did. Then he scooped his hat from the floor. So he was a genius too. Ha!

"There has to be something here, though," I said, staring at the files in front of us. I could just sense it, and I was sure the other three could sense it as well. What were the chances the four of us were born in the same week, at the same time, and were here at Power Academy together? It seemed too strange to be a simple coincidence.

"I agree, but it's not helping us find our stuff. That's for sure," Ellie said, reading my mind. For once, she made sense. We could try to figure out the connection all night, but that wouldn't bring us any closer to finding Pickle and the other hidden items.

We stared at one another, not knowing where to look next.

"So, we've hit another dead end." Sam sighed in exasperation.

"I guess we're stuck here all summer after all," Ellie said, slouching down in the corner chair. "Let's just go find Larriby and tell her we give up. We'll just ask for our stuff back, and demand that she tell us what's up with those note cards," she added.

Sam's hand reached for the doorknob.

"No way! Wait," I pleaded. "You seriously want to give up now?" They were nuts! I couldn't believe they would give in to Larriby and greasy Grimeley so fast.

Nobody moved.

We stared at one other, waiting for inspiration to strike. I looked over at Ellie and the huge bookcase situated on the wall behind her. The familiarity of it hit me. "Stand up," I insisted, jumping forward.

"But I need a little rest," Ellie complained, looking down at her now paint-chipped nails and frowned.

"Seriously. Stand up," I demanded, steering Ellie up and away from the bookcase.

I used all my weight to push the chair out of the way.

"Poppy, what are you doing?" Logan asked, giving Sam a strange look.

"The bookcase." I motioned to them. "Help me slide it, guys," I said, struggling with it alone.

"Let's do it," Sam said while puffing out his chest.

"Step back," Logan said to me and winked. "We got this."

Ellie and I giggled together. They were totally trying to be macho boys.

Sam was on one side of the shelf, and Logan on the other. Of course a few pieces of hair had fallen over Logan's green eyes. But I was beginning to like the whole rugged hair-in-face look he had going on. It was cute.

"On three," Logan said. "One … two … three."

With each grunt from the boys, the bookshelf slid farther and farther away from its position against the wall.

And then they saw what was hidden behind it. I gave a knowing smile.

Logan's eyes bulged out of his head, "Nooooo way!"

"Awesome."

"I want a hidden compartment in my bedroom," said Ellie in her typical world-revolves-around-Ellie fashion. I laughed.

I knew then exactly why Miss Maggie assigned that lesson. She wanted me—us—to succeed.

"Check this out." Logan pointed to the upper-left-hand corner of the built-in shelf where a mini flat-screen television sat.

"Why would she have a TV hidden away in here?"

"Quick, find the remote!" Ellie chirped.

"Really, guys?" Sam sighed, aiming his finger up at the

screen. The TV buzzed on. Okay. His powers were so not lame.

"Oh, man."

"Oh. My. Gosh," Ellie said dramatically.

From the angle I stood (due to my height), I couldn't quite make out what was on the screen. I moved to get a better view. And then I saw it.

"Surveillance? Really?"

I jumped on the chair to get a better look, and pushed a few curly strands of red hair from my face. On the screen was what seemed to be a storage shed. In fact, it looked just like the shed my dad has in our back yard where he stores the lawnmower, snowplow thingy, and other tools. Unlike my dad's, though, this one looked like it had been through World War II. Panels of siding were missing, there was a ginormous hole in the roof, and boards were nailed up over all the windows.

I swallowed hard and gestured to the dilapidated building. "Do you think that Pickle's in there?"

Sam nodded. "If Old Lady Larriby's going to hide anything anywhere, this is where it would be," he said, using his Wednesday power to turn off the TV. "I think that is where *all* of our stuff is hidden. Why else would crazy Larriby have it under surveillance?" That woman was just plain nuts.

I shrugged and stared at everyone else, hoping someone

would make the next call. Not that I minded saving the day or anything.

"Well, let's go get our stuff," Sam finally said.

Ellie twisted strands of hair between her fingers. "But we don't even know where this place is. Plus, it looks kind of scar—"

"Are you forgetting who the veteran P.A. student is?" Sam asked, pointing at his chest. "I know right where it is." He motioned toward the door. "Follow me."

Logan's warm hand grabbed mine as he helped me down and off the chair.

"Thanks," I muttered quietly, and hoped he wouldn't see the pink in my cheeks.

We quietly left Headmistress Larriby's office and were led down a hallway from the brilliant light emanating from Sam's hand. His power was really coming in handy tonight. No pun intended.

"So, where exactly are we going?" I asked once we silently exited out the back door of the academy and was positive nobody could hear.

Our eyes followed his outstretched arm. "Out there."

I gulped, unsure if finding our stuff really was worth this.

Sam continued, "To the haunted forest we go."

Chapter Eighteen

Ellie's breath came out in short bursts as we hiked through the supposedly haunted forest. I turned to see if she was okay. Her wide eyes gave away just how terrified she really was.

Sure, it was late at night. Plus, there was that rumor about the kid who got lost out here forever (which I totally hoped was just that—a rumor). Add in the fact that this place was once a crazy experimental insane asylum or something like it. Really, if you put the ingredients together, this entire academy was a recipe for haunted creepiness. But I found it to be kind of exciting.

"You don't *actually* believe this place is haunted, do you?" Sam teased Ellie.

"Maybe," she stated meekly.

"Boo!" Logan jumped toward Ellie.

"Ahhhhhhhh!" she shrieked.

I chuckled. How could she not see that coming?

"I can protect you," Sam bellowed, nudging Logan and me out of the way so he could get to Ellie. His arm awkwardly dangled over her shoulder.

Ellie wiggled away from his grasp. "Um … okay." She sent me a *save me, Poppy* kind of look, and I swore I heard her say those words aloud.

"Sam, how much farther do we have to go?" I asked, trying to get his googly eyes off of her.

"It shouldn't be that far away," he said, turning toward me.

Ellie wiggled out from under his arm. *Thank You*, she mouthed, and rolled her eyes at Sam.

Sam's light guided us on the way. We really would be lost without him.

"Are you doing okay?" Logan asked, throwing his arm around my shoulder.

I smiled. Thank goodness it was too dark for him to see just how big of a smile it was. "I think so," I said apprehensively. To be perfectly honest, the darkness didn't really scare me that much. Just as long as Sam gave us some sort of light, I would be fine.

"Guys! I think that I see something over there." Ellie pointed to a shadowy outline twenty or so yards away.

"Can we get some more light?"

A brighter flashlight-like light shot out from Sam's pointer finger. "No problem." I'd never, ever seen a Wednesday shoot light that far. It was more than awesome! Why was he even here?

"That's it! That's it!" Ellie yelled, and began running, well, more like stumbling toward it. With each step, her black kitten heels let go of the mud and they clicked back against her feet.

As we got closer, I could hear a faint whimpering coming from inside. *Pickle, I'm coming.*

"We need to find a way in," Logan said.

Since Sam provided the only light, we all had to stick together. Ellie grasped the hood of my sweatshirt until I was practically choking. "Lighten up on the grip," I said. She did and then latched on to my arm. I could hear her teeth rattling in my ear.

As we pushed our way through the overgrown bushes and weeds surrounding the base of the building, Pickle's whines got louder and louder.

I needed to get to her.

After circling the entire dilapidated shed, we realized that unless we had a key to unlock the front padlock over the door, there was no way in.

I looked over to see Logan's face smashed up against a board. "There's a hole in this board over here." He waved us over to him. And then his voice rose in excitement, "I think I see Pickle!"

I shoved him out of the way, probably a little too hard, and pressed my face up against the musty board. Gross.

"Pickle," I whisper-yelled.

Her cute little eyes looked through the black wire crate she was held in, and up toward me. From what I could see, there was a bowl of water and food on one side of the crate, and a blanket on the other. *Thank goodness she's not starving,* I thought to myself. I knew deep down that Larriby wouldn't actually hurt her. Next to Pickle was a soccer ball that I assumed was Logan's, and a black box that probably held a clarinet.

"Do you see my bracelet?" Ellie asked, now hanging on to Logan's arm for dear life. Sam shot him a death stare.

"I think so," I said, noticing a small pink box that, by color alone, could only be Ellie's.

"Girls, stand guard," Logan commanded, pulling away from Ellie. "Come on, Sam." He pushed his finger in the hole and squeezed another finger in and around one of the looser boards. "Get the other side," Logan demanded.

Sam finally moved, stood on the other side of the board, and did the same thing as Logan. Their attempt at pulling off the board didn't produce the same results as their attempt to move the bookcase in Headmistress Larriby's office a little while ago.

"Shoot," Sam said, looking down at his swollen red fingers. "Not gonna happen."

Logan's hands looked the same.

"Can't you just disappear and reappear in there?" Sam asked.

Logan gave him a you-are-such-an-idiot look. "I'm a Friday, not a Tuesday. I don't teleport, remember?"

"Oh, yeah." Sam nodded at Logan. "Let's look for another way in."

"You mean, you're just gonna leave us here … alone?" Ellie asked, digging her sharp nails into my arm now.

That was exactly what they meant.

We waited in the pitch-black scariness while Logan and Sam did one more lap around the building.

"Eeep! What was that?" Ellie jumped back and looked down toward her feet. Her purse had fallen. "Uh … oh." I rolled my eyes at *her* this time.

"Come on, guys—"

"Shhhh."

And they were back.

"Looks like this is our only way in," Logan stated firmly, gesturing toward the loose board over the window. "And it's not budging for us."

All sets of eyes were on me.

"What?" I asked.

They still stared. I knew what had to be done, and they

were right.

Okay. I guess it was my turn to *prove* my power. I mean, Ellie showed us all that she could control the use of her power by NOT listening to nostril-man Mr. Grimeley's mind when retrieving the key code. Thanks to Logan's Friday power we got into Headmistress Larriby's office without getting caught by greasy Grimeley. And even though Sam was already pretty much the master of his Wednesday power, we definitely couldn't have gotten this far without his help.

I thought about how I would spend my summer if we got out of here. Hanging out with Veronica and Pickle, maybe even Ellie. Eating ice cream at Novalicious down the street. Celebrating my birthday. Camping with my mom and dad.

"Ewww. You actually *like* camping?" Ellie interrupted my thought. "And those gross bugs and stuff. Ick!"

Had she done that four days ago, I would have been annoyed. I smiled this time. "You *were* doing so well, Ellie." We laughed together like friends.

I turned back toward the shed. "I can do this," I said, surprising myself with confidence.

Everyone took four totally obvious, gigantic steps back.

"C'mon guys!" I pleaded. But I guess I couldn't blame them. After all, they had seen the disastrous results of my Monday power before, even if I had been so much closer to getting it right lately.

Although I tried to keep my mind totally clear, I couldn't stop thinking about the first accident with Ellie's headband, spaghetti on Dad's bald head, Pickle's brush tangled in my necklaces, Miss Maggie's water glass crashing to the floor, Logan's gross stuffing, Ellie's nose paper cut, the book case, and how my powers had failed with each of those attempts. But then, I thought of Pickle, and how I wanted more than anything else in the world to get her out of this terrible place and get us home for the rest of the summer. More than that, I wanted to show clothes-too-tight Larriby and whomever she was talking to the other day that we could totally do this!

Of course Headmistress Larriby would leave this up to me, I said to myself, thinking back to that first day of Power Academy that seriously felt like forever ago when I made her crash to the floor, and the way she treated us since. I could do this.

I slowly lifted up my arm and pointed to the loose side of the board. *Concentrate, Poppy. Concentrate.* It was so quiet behind me that I could have sworn that the others weren't even breathing. The quiet was broken by Pickle's whimpering, though, and that motivated me to go on.

I focused on one of the screws that held up the two-inch thick wooden plank. I didn't want it to pull so fast that it shot out and stabbed someone, so I imagined it turning ever so slowly.

Turn, turn, turn, I thought, pointing as hard as I possibly could. And the screw did it. It turned. Yes! One step closer.

My heart began to race a little faster.

"I'm getting it gu—"

There was shuffling behind me. "Poppy, you'd better hurry," Ellie screeched like a mouse.

Sam took the light away from the board and shined it toward Power Academy. I turned to see two figures quickly making their way toward us.

I didn't realize Headmistress Larriby could move that fast.

"Poppy, quick," Logan said, running up to the board, attempting to pull at the corner where the screw was almost out. The wooden plank still wasn't budging.

Pickle's whines were getting louder.

Then I focused on the lower corner of the plank. *Turn, turn, turn.* Again, the screw did what I said. Awesome!

"They're almost here," Ellie shouted frantically, and even higher pitched than before.

Logan's face contorted as he strained to pull at the corner of the board. "Just a little farther, Poppy," he choked.

There were at least two more nails to go before this thing would budge. I didn't have time to unscrew them.

"Get back, Logan," I ordered.

With no questions asked, he jumped behind me.

"Hurry up, Poppy!"

I concentrated harder than I had ever had to before. *Come on. Come on. Come on.*

The board wasn't moving.

"They're getting closer."

It was totally up to me now. I had to do it. I heard Ellie's hysterical cries from behind me. *Come on. Come on.* I concentrated. *Just snap!* I could hear the footsteps and shuffling getting closer.

"Hurry!"

Come on. Snap! And just when I thought my efforts were useless—*CRACK*. The board snapped in two and wooden fragments flew to the sides.

"Did you just do that?" Logan asked while clearing the rest of the debris from the window.

"I think so," I said, astonished and super excited that it did completely what I wanted it to. My Monday power worked! But it wasn't over yet—we didn't actually have our stuff.

Logan moved back into the brush against the building and got down on one knee. "Get on, now."

In one swift movement, I jumped on Logan's knee and hopped through the window—the window that I just made free with my Monday power. Awesome!

Sam dove into the air and did some sort of martial arts

roll into a smooth landing on the shed's floor. Strange, yet impressive.

I could see Mr. Grimeley not too far behind Ellie. "Hurry up, Ellie," I said while reaching toward her hand.

Ellie's foot made it to Logan's knee. Greasy Grimeley was like ten feet away. But right before Ellie was able to push herself off of Logan's knee, Logan disappeared. The lower half of Ellie's body was still dangling outside. I heard her heel *plop* to the damp ground below.

"Reach," I said.

Her fingers grabbed on to mine. I pulled as hard as I could, but she wasn't moving.

"Ewww, ouch," Ellie whimpered.

"Oh, no, you're not," Mr. Grimeley screeched, clutching on to the bottom of her black yoga pants.

It was like a tug-of-war competition between Mr. Grimeley and me, and Ellie was the rope.

I concentrated on Mr. Grimeley's hand, trying not to be distracted by the nostrils that looked extra large in the moonlight tonight.

I focused harder than ever again. *Nose. Nose. Nose.*

"Get her!" I heard Larriby yell from behind him.

Nose. Nose. Nose.

And just like that, Mr. Grimeley's hand shot up and away from Ellie's pants. His pointer finger went right up his left nostril.

Headmistress Larriby was almost to the shed now. My hand lifted and pointed toward the two nasty adults a few feet away. *Ground!* And on that command, Mr. Grimeley stumbled backward into Larriby, and they both crashed to the dirt below.

"Wow! Nice work, Poppy," Ellie said as I pulled her the rest of the way in.

Sam turned his flashlight-finger down toward Headmistress Larriby. Her beet-red cheeks puffed up with every deep inhalation she took.

"I have never," she paused to catch her breath, "in my life, had anyone," more heavy breathing, "come this close to leaving *my* Academy … early!" Mrs. Larriby's voice boomed angrily, even through all that panting.

The four of us ran to the other side of the shed, as far away from that window as possible.

Sam grabbed his clarinet, Logan his soccer ball, and Ellie found her bracelet. Pickle's tail wagged like I had never seen it wag before as I tried to unlatch the cage. I fumbled with it.

"Don't let her get that stupid little dog," Larriby shouted as Mr. Grimeley climbed through the window. "They can't—"

Grimeley's arm raised and I watched as his eyes burned into Pickle. "Noo!" I shouted.

I could barely wrap my mind around everything that

happened in the next few seconds. Heck, I don't think any of us could wrap our minds around it. Suddenly, Logan disappeared and then instantly reappeared behind Mr. Grimeley. I could feel my eyes bulging from their sockets. Did I really just see that? Logan hadn't just disappeared. He had teleported. Logan, a disappearing Friday had done something only reserved for Tuesdays.

"Awesome," he said in shock, while still managing to pull greasy-nostril-man Grimeley's arms behind his back, distracting him so he couldn't use his Monday power at all.

At that point, Mrs. Larriby had pulled her large self through the shed window. Our eyes met. Before I could even move, she was charging toward the cage that held Pickle. I panicked and froze, and then something even stranger happened. In less than an instant, I watched Ellie's hand rise up and point toward the metal cage holding Pickle. Before I could even blink, the cage slid sharply to the left just as Headmistress Larriby came close to reaching it. What the heck? Did Ellie just…

Ellie opened and closed her eyes hard a few times in disbelief.

"Now!" I yelled, somehow knowing what Sam wanted to do next.

An intense stream of light from his finger flashed in Larriby's face. Temporarily blinded, she stumbled backward, and then regained balance. She started toward

Ellie and the pink jewelry box that was now in her hand.

"Do something!" Ellie yelled, but I was one-hundred-percent positive that her mouth didn't move. I had definitely just read her mind.

I knew that she was talking to me, so I pointed toward Logan's soccer ball. *Hit her!* And just like that—it did. The ball smacked into Larriby's forehead and she stumbled a few more steps backward.

"Quick, Sam!" Sam rushed over and helped me hold her huge body down. It definitely took two of us.

"Now that's what you call teamwork," Logan yelled, holding Grimeley in a headlock now.

"I got her," Sam said, holding Larriby to the ground.

Pickle ran to me, and I smiled as her tongue licked the side of my face. "I missed you, too, girl."

The four of us stood over the defeated duo that was clothes-too-tight Larriby and greasy-nostril-man Grimeley with our found belongings in hand. "We've passed your stupid challenge," Ellie yelled.

"Yeah," the boys shouted.

Ellie smiled and nodded at me.

"Now you'd better tell us what the heck is going on!" I demanded, taking the words right out of Ellie's head.

Chapter Nineteen

I bent down toward the furry circle in my lap, and gave Pickle a gentle rub behind her ears. Her eyes slowly closed. I sighed. It was nice to have her back.

I looked up to see the tight-lipped Headmistress Larriby sitting across her large oak desk from the four of us. She had our information cards in her hand and was twirling them in her fingers so quickly that flicks of fluorescent yellow highlighter marks flittered around like fireflies.

We needed answers about the whole thing that just happened in that shed, and over the last hour, no one wanted to give us any. We begged Larriby and Grimeley to talk after we succeeded in the challenge, but they hadn't spoken one word to us at all.

A loud knock on the wooden door broke the silence.

"Come in," Headmistress Larriby shouted.

Mr. Grimeley escorted in a tall, blond, lanky woman dressed in a red fitted pantsuit.

"Mayor Masters." Headmistress Larriby's chair creaked as she pushed herself up. "It's a pleasure to—"

"Sit back down, Mayella. There's no need to suck up to me now," the well-dressed woman demanded.

I laughed inside.

"That's her," I heard Logan say. At this point, I wasn't entirely sure if he said it aloud or if I read it from his head.

"That's *her*," he said again. It took me a moment to realize what he meant. Oh! That was the woman who the boys overheard speaking to Mrs. Larriby about "the girls holding them back." Well, we *girls* sure showed her.

On that thought, Mayor Masters' head whipped around to me. "Poppy Rose Mayberry, as much as you try to keep your thoughts to yourself, it rarely works," Mayor Masters, an apparent Thursday said while locking her eyes with mine. "And yes. You ladies did show me!" Her red lips curled up and into a warm, somehow familiar smile.

Phew!

"I would like to speak with these four." Mayor Masters nodded toward Logan, Sam, Ellie, and me. "Alone," she emphasized.

On that cue, Grimeley shuffled out of the office and Headmistress Mayella Larriby pushed herself up from her chair and followed. Mrs. Larriby's first name was Mayella? Seemed like such a sweet name for such a sour person.

"We'll be discussing your behavior later," Mayor Masters shouted to Headmistress Larriby. She gingerly lifted her hand and pointed toward the door. It slammed behind Larriby's big butt. Mayor Masters was not only a mind-reading Thursday, she was a Monday as well.

What was going on?

Mayor Masters looked toward the fur ball in my lap and frowned. Pickle. "I had no idea the headmistress stole a live dog as part of her challenge," Mayor Masters said while shaking her head. Clothes-too-tight Larriby was going to get in trouble because of Pickle. "I was unaware that this item was a living thing, however," she said, pointing at Pickle. I was pretty sure the disapproving tone in her last words was directed toward me.

I should never have brought Pickle here in the first place.

Mayor Masters unbuttoned her suit jacket and then delicately sat in Mrs. Larriby's chair. Although she looked mini standing next to the plump Headmistress Larriby, she looked even smaller against the oversized seat. We waited long enough to know what's been going on, and I had a feeling that we were about to find out.

"We've had our eyes on the four of you for quite some time now," she broke the silence, speaking matter-of-factly.

"Who is *we?*" Logan said, pushing a few strands of hair from his face.

"Well …" She cleared her throat and looked between Ellie and me. "Of course there's Principal Wible at Nova Elementary."

That made sense. He did send Ellie and me here in the first place.

"All of your instructors here at Power Academy, including Maggie Masters," she cleared her throat and looked at me, "my daughter."

My eyes lit up. "You're Miss Maggie's mom?"

"Yes, dear," she answered, chuckling.

"But she—"

Mayor Masters fidgeted in her seat. "She studied in England and lived there for years—to see how people live without our special talents." She smiled. "She just returned two months ago," Mayor Masters explained.

Ahh. Since Mayor Masters was her mother, then it was no wonder Miss Maggie had singled me out so often. I thought about her continuous cheers and tips, and the airplane note she sent me. And then a trigger went off. That note she had written seemed strange to me, but I had pushed if out of my head. The airplane had read *Embrace your powers*. Powers. With an *S*. Plural. I smiled to myself.

"I'll explain that in a bit, Poppy," Mayor Masters said, reading my thoughts. Miss Maggie definitely had her mom's warm smile.

"What about clothes-too-ti—" Sam started. Logan nudged his side, and rephrased his question. "I mean Headmistress Larriby and Mr. Grimeley?"

"Of course they work for me," she said through more chuckles. "Mayella and William do a nice job of scaring the students into mastering powers." She sighed. "And they did a particularly nice job of helping the four of you find your true potential." She glanced down at the cards once more and then back up at us.

Mayor Masters motioned us to pull our chairs closer to the desk. We did.

"But wh—"

"Ellie. I will explain everything," Mayor Masters cut her off. "Just give me the chance."

Ellie sighed. "What-ev."

As rude as Ellie could be, I totally understood her frustration in this situation. There was no doubt about it, just a few hours ago she had moved Pickle's cage without a nudge, push, or anything. Something that only Mondays can do. And then there was Logan's teleporting, and my mind reading. And Sam had super strong Wednesday powers. We were all in need of an explanation.

"As you all have probably noticed, Power Academy is not only intended for those who are behind in their weekday powers, like you all originally thought," Mayor Masters said as her thin fingers spread our information cards out in front of her. "That was simply the pretense under which you were sent here," she continued with a broad smile. "It worked out perfectly in your cases, however, as each of you did need some work with your dominant power." She sent a wink our way.

Dominant power? What did she mean by that?

"Yes. It is true that the larger purpose of Power Academy is to assist the struggling students in catching up with other Weekdays in Nova—those students in your power-intensive classes, for example. But," she scooted her chair even closer to the desk and hushed her voice, "the other objective is to target a certain, *special* group of students." Her eyes lit up at the mention of the word special. Her rounded fingernails tapped on our cards.

"It has to do with our birthdays, doesn't it?" I asked, already knowing the answer.

"Yes, Poppy. It does." She smiled. "And what exactly do you notice about them?"

"We're all born in the same week at the same exact time," Logan spoke up, pointing to the highlighted line on his card.

"Exactly. 11:59 p.m."

Ellie scrunched her face. "But I don't get it."

Mayor Masters went on. "Individuals born in Nova just on the cusp of another weekday have the potential to possess more than one power."

Whoa!

Mayor Masters sat up straighter in her chair, which seemed impossible considering she had perfect posture as it was.

"Like tonight," Logan's voice rose in excitement. "Like when I teleported."

"Yes, Logan." Mayor Masters pursed her lips.

"Or like when I totally moved Pickle's cage with my mind?"

"Yes, Ellie." Mayor Masters' lips loosened into a slight smile. "Or you, Poppy," she said, tapping her pointer finger to her head.

So, I had been able to read Ellie's mind after all! This was just too crazy to believe though. How was it possible?

Mayor Masters' face became serious. "This will take some processing," she said, taking a deep breath.

Sam crossed his arms in front of his chest and tilted his head to the side. "I think we can handle it."

I knew we could handle it.

Mayor Masters nodded. "If you are born right on the cusp of two days, as you all were, you have the potential of not only possessing the power of the dominant day, but you also have the potential of inheriting a power from one of your parents." She paused, giving us a moment to comprehend what she just said.

Mayor Masters now concentrated on Sam. "Since your mother is also a Wednesday, your Wednesday powers are doubly strong."

Sam puffed his chest out and smiled broadly. No wonder he could do all that crazy light-electricity stuff better than even my Dad. And he was an awesome Wednesday.

This was just so … well … unreal. Not only could I move things with my Monday power, but I could read minds like my mom does with her Thursday power. Craziness!

Mayor Masters spoke carefully. "It's quite unusual to have four of you born at the time, and never have we had four different cusp students here at the academy at once …" Her index finger pointed toward the cards in front of her, and just like that, they stacked into a pile without her having to touch a single one at all.

We all gasped.

"You're like us, too?" Logan asked.

"It seems so, doesn't it?" she said. "When I first encountered my second weekday power, my cusp power, I was mystified and honestly—a bit scared. Here I was born a Monday—just getting used to my Monday powers, and then all of a sudden I'm sitting in sixth-grade history class hearing millions of thoughts from the students sitting around me like a true Thursday." She sighed. "Talk about confused!"

Three of us chuckled, while Ellie just stared ahead.

"I still don't get it," she said with her jaw hung open. Poor Ellie.

"Don't you see, Ellie? You have more than your own weekday power to master; you have your mother's power to master as well."

"You mean I'm, like, kinda a Monday too?" Her voice screeched in excitement, and then quieted. "Like my Mom," she said to herself, but loud enough for me to hear.

Mayors Masters cupped her hand over Ellie's and nodded. "Yes, dear."

"Each year we create reasons to invite those like the four of you to Power Academy. Rarely do we even have one cusp student."

The four of us listened intently.

"As I said before, most of you needed to work on your dominant power as well, so it worked out perfectly. As for the other cusp power—it's best that you discovered your talents in a safe, controlled environment." She paused and looked around. "Here. We were hoping that if we put enough pressure on you, then you would not only demonstrate the mastery of your true weekday power, but show a hint of your other one." She smiled. "And after hearing about what happened with the Headmaster and her assistant, it worked better than we anticipated." She laughed. "All four of you found your cusp power quickly—" She stopped, but the strained look on her face told me that she wanted to say more.

"Go on," I urged, sensing she was going to say something important.

But she shook whatever that was away and spoke. "I'm just sorry that Headmistress Larriby and Mr. Grimeley had to be so ... well, so—"

"Mean, nasty, rude, cruel," Ellie interrupted, saying out loud what we all thought. "I can go on it you'd like," she said, batting her eyelashes.

"She gets the point," Logan said, rolling his eyes.

"And I will be addressing their behavior," Mayor Masters stated firmly. "But, know that I did advise them to put some additional pressure on you." She leaned back in her chair and chuckled. "And you two boys." She shook her head side to side, and laughed louder. "The conversation you overheard was just what the four of you needed to give you that extra little push."

"You set that up?" Logan asked and then looked at Sam.

"Let's just say you needed some motivation." Her eyes quickly darted to Ellie.

So, Mayor Masters and Larriby were simply acting out a script when the boys overheard them. They wanted us to believe that Ellie and I were the reasons we wouldn't leave early—just to give us more of a reason to master our powers. They were good. Really good.

Sam jumped out of his seat. "Oh, man! This is too cool!

I can't wait to tell—"

"No one," Mayor Masters demanded. She tightly closed her eyes and then opened them again. Her voice softened. "Not yet, at least." She scooted in closer—even though I was pretty sure there wasn't any more room for her to do so. "We are unsure how the general public will react to the knowledge of dual powers, and so it's something that must be worked with delicately." Her lips pursed again. "I'm sure you understand."

We nodded.

"So, who else knows about the two-power thing then?" I asked.

"Just those who I mentioned earlier, your parents, and, of course the others who are like you all."

Ellie shot up straight. "There are others?"

Mayor Masters laughed. "Ellie. It's quite possible that other Nova residents are born at the stroke of midnight. You see, there are only ten of us that we know of at this point."

Only ten? And if we have this crazy cusp power ability, who knows what else is out there?

"Exactly, Poppy," Mayor Masters said, reading me again. "If that's possible, who knows what else is." Mayor Masters stood up. "But that's something we at Nova Power Corporation are trying to work out."

Mayor Masters grabbed our files and slid them under

her arm. "I will be in contact with each of you toward the end of the summer to discuss the next steps."

What was she talking about? "Next steps?" I asked.

"You four have much to learn over the next year, and the first part of that learning process occurs at the beginning of sixth grade." Her heels clicked against the tiled floor as she made her way toward the door.

"You will all be enrolled at Nova Middle." Mayor Masters nodded toward Logan. "Even you."

"Awesome, man." Sam slapped a high five to Logan. "No more home school!"

She reached for the doorknob. "In the meantime—enjoy the rest of your summer. Although you should focus on your true weekday power, you will find your secondary power becoming stronger and stronger every day." She smiled and opened the office door. "Work with it, but …" She turned and her voice lowered. "But be careful not to share this information with others. We are still working on what this means exactly for those like us."

Just like that, Mayor Masters was gone.

"This is like the craziest thing EVER!" Ellie grinned from ear to ear. She always wanted to be a Monday … and now she kinda was.

Logan rubbed his eyes. "I know. Let's just get our stuff together and get the heck outta here. We can focus on all this when we get back home."

"Mmhm," I agreed. There were so many unanswered questions, but my number-one priority was getting me and Pickle the heck home. Hopefully, Mom and Dad could explain the rest.

But gosh. It took me long enough to get decent with my Monday power. I can't even imagine how long it will take to perfect my Thursday one.

Chapter Twenty

"I can't believe this was a set-up!" Ellie said, grinning from ear to ear. "And to think, I have been a Monday all along!" Ellie hadn't stopped smiling since our conversation with Mayor Masters. She definitely had a reason to. "And Mayor Masters said that our parents knew about it!" She pursed her lips in confusion. "Then, why?" her voice trailed off. She and her mother obviously had some things to discuss this summer.

"No kidding! And I'm a Thursday just like you," I said, breaking the sudden tension.

Ellie turned toward me and spoke matter-of-factly. "You know, I knew there was something strange going on the whole time," she said, flicking a few strands of hair behind her neck. She turned back around and packed more pink shirts into her luggage.

I laughed to myself. It was typical Ellie-style to act as if she knew about our secret powers all along. Looking back, though, I realized that I could have put it together sooner. Things added up. First, the way my Mom acted before I left for Power Academy. The few instances where I thought I read people's minds—especially that confusing conversation between Ellie and me in our dorm room. I guess the paint fumes didn't get to her, after all. The strange looks between Larriby and Grimeley. The note with Miss Maggie. Sam's super intense Wednesday power. Although it stunk being here for the beginning of summer, I sure was glad we found out about our second power here— together—with Logan, Sam, and yes … even Ellie.

But one thing was still gnawing at me—sure, we were all born on the cusp, but was there something more to the fact we were all born in the same exact week? It all seemed too coincidental, like there was more to this whole situation. Hopefully I would find ou—

"Can you help me with this?" Ellie asked, breaking me from my thoughts. She was attempting to zip up her tote overflowing with kitten heels and flats.

"No problem!" I shrugged. "After all …" I hesitated, deciding whether or not to say what I was thinking. I figured I would say it before Ellie read it though. "That's what friends do, right?" I asked, unsure of how she would react. Sure. We had overcome a lot of drama the last few weeks—years worth—but would the niceness last?

She paused and her eyes met mine. "Yeah, Poppy ... that's exactly what friends do," she said, pushing together the two zipper edges. With a quick flick of my wrist, the zipper teeth buzzed together. Ellie swooped Pickle up and rubbed her little tan and gray head before handing her over to me.

"Let's get home," she said.

Chapter Twenty-One

Pickle, Logan, Sam, Ellie, Mayor Masters, Headmistress Larriby, Mr. Grimeley, and I stood outside the main entrance of P.A. waiting for our parents to arrive. Well, not really together. The three adults stood a good ten feet away from us, but I could tell by the way Mayor Masters's arms were waving around and the looks on all of their faces that she was not happy with Larriby and Grimeley.

"Unacceptable," "they're just kids," "probation," "a dog?" and other such phrases flew from Mayor Masters's mouth. Headmistress Larriby just stood there in her ill-fitting red body suit, which made her look like the largest tomato on the face of the earth, wincing at every other word.

"You'd better believe that I'll be keeping a close eye on

the two of you," Mayor Masters continued nice and loudly. The four of us giggled. It was good to see the two of them get put in their place. It reminded me of the way Larriby yelled at me that first day in the library after that chair incident (which was a total accident by the way!). What goes around comes around.

Sam's dad was the first to show. Mr. Bricker was exactly as I had imagined him to be. He wore the same exact cowboy hat Sam had on. To go along with the hat, he wore a leather vest and cowboy boots with those spur thingies that clinked and clanged with each step he took packing up the car.

"See ya in a few months, guys," Sam said brightly. He and Logan shook hands, which still was funny to me, and then he moved on to Ellie. Before she could even dodge him, his arms wrapped tightly around her.

"Uh … okay … bye," she said, pushing him off. But when she turned toward me, it was easy to see that she was trying to hide a huge grin. Sam smirked, waved to me, and jumped in his father's truck.

Ellie was the next to go. Her lips twitched a bit. Her attempt at hiding a frown was unsuccessful. Poor Ellie. Neither of her parents even ventured out here to pick her up. The same chauffeur who dropped her off opened the town car's door for her now.

"Tah-tah!" she yipped, wiggling her fingers at Logan.

She took a step toward me, then hesitated, obviously weighing her next move. Her mind was made up. She launched herself forward at me. Her skinny arms wrapped around my shoulders. "I am so glad to have you as a friend, Poppy." I wasn't sure if she said it aloud, or if it as in her head, but there was no denying that she meant it.

She pet Pickle's head one more time, hopped into the luxurious car, and smiled at me until the tinted windows rolled up and over her eyes.

And then there were two. Logan and me. It was a little awkward.

I pushed the toe of my gladiator sandal around in the dirt.

"Maybe we could hang out over the summer or something," Logan said, breaking the silence.

"I'd like that," I said, and glanced up to notice once again that a few strands of hair fell into his face. I lifted my finger and concentrated on those few pieces. *Move. Move. Move.* And it worked! Just like that, the hairs shifted far enough to the left that I could see every bit of his forest-green eyes.

"Thanks."

I was so distracted by Logan for a minute that I almost didn't notice Mom and Dad pull up. I swooped Pickle in my arms and ran over to greet them.

"Poppy!" They both wrapped their arms tightly around

me. "We are just so proud of our precious Monday," Dad said, rubbing my head and messing up the bun Ellie had helped me perfect this earlier this morning. Ugh. But that didn't really matter—it felt good to be around them again.

"Our precious Thursday, too!" Mom said, giving me that proud-mom smile that I had missed so much.

I waved to Mayor Masters and, yes, even Headmistress Larriby and greasy nostril-man Grimeley, too, and hopped in our car.

Just as we were about to pull away, Logan knocked on my window. I rolled it down, and before I could figure out what was happening I felt his lips press into my cheek. My freckles burned with excitement. "See you around, Poppy!" he said through a smirk. And being the cute Friday that he is, he disappeared right then and there before I even had a chance to respond.

And with that—I was on my way home.

Chapter Twenty-Two

After those tremendously long days at Power Academy, the rest of the summer totally flew. There was only one more week until I would officially be a sixth grader at Nova Middle. Unbelievable!

Today was like most of the other summer days. Veronica and I sat by her parents' humongous pool, sipping on ice-cold lemonades, reading magazines, and talking our heads off. Pickle drifted on a raft in the middle of the water. What a diva dog! Her bright pink swimsuit glimmered in the hot sun. The swimsuit that was a gift from, guess who? Ellie—we were totally on good terms now, and we had been ever since our talk at Power Academy.

Although she could be a prissy pretty-girl, she truly had a good heart and we had much more in common than we thought. It was hard to believe that just a few months ago we were pretty much enemies. It was even harder to believe that just a few months ago I could barely call myself a Monday, and now I was a Thursday, too!

Just as I was about to flip the page in my *Girls' World Magazine*, I heard a buzzing sound coming from the lounge chair like ten feet over. My cell phone.

As a combination *congrats on passing P.A. early, good luck at Nova Middle,* and *Happy eleventh birthday* gift, my parents got me a phone. The only people that I knew who had phones of their own were Logan and Ellie. And Ellie was definitely not texting me because she and Celia were tanning just two lounge chairs over.

"Are you going to get that?" Ellie asked without moving her lips, sending a knowing smile my way. Her fluorescent-pink nails pointed toward the phone.

Now, I could have gotten up and taken a few steps over to reach it, but decided that I might as well use my Monday power. I concentrated on the plastic purple phone lifting gently from the lounge, floating toward me, and then landing safely into my hands. But instead, at like ten-thousand miles an hour, it flew off the chair and splashed into …

Just kidding! What I imagined actually happened just like I wanted it to. The phone gently landed in the palm of my hands. I swiped the unlock button with my thumb (I'm not *that* lazy, after all), and read my first text.

Logan: See u in a few days.

I smiled. So many awesome things had happened this summer. I had totally mastered my Monday power. My super-secret Thursday mind reading was getting better and better. Mom's not that good at censoring her thoughts, so I kind of already knew about the cell phone gift before I opened it. But most awesome of all, Ellie and I were now friends—real friends. Veronica, Ellie, Celia, and I had spent most of the summer together. There was so much to be happy about! I just couldn't wait until Mayor Masters filled us in on the plan for next year—whatever that would be.

I sank back into the lounge chair, took a sip of lemonade, glanced at my friends, new and old, and smiled at Ellie as I read her mind. I nodded in agreement—sixth grade was going to be pretty much the most fantabulous year ever!

ACKNOWLEDGEMENTS

First, a huge thank you to my parents for their love and support throughout my life. Thank you both for always believing in me!

Thank you to my family, friends, and colleagues (both former and current), for their love and support as I wrote POPPY.

I am thankful that Quinlan Lee pulled POPPY out of the slush pile a few years ago, giving me the confidence in Poppy and her story to push forward through revisions. I am forever grateful for the day that Bill Contardi agreed to be my agent. His professionalism, industry savvy, and ability to always say the right thing is all I could ask for in an agent. Thanks to the entire team at Brandt & Hochman Literary Agency.

Thank you to everyone at Georgia McBride Media Group, Month9Books, and Tantrum Books for their excitement over this book and for welcoming me into the GMMG family. Thank you to my amazing editor Tara Creel, and a huge thanks to Georgia McBride for making my dreams come true!

Thank you to my wonderful debut brothers and sisters

at The Sweet Sixteens, and a special shout out to my Sixteen to Read gals! Your enthusiasm has been fantabulous!

To my students, readers, bloggers, librarians, teachers, and fans – you all are awesome, and I am so happy you've supported me and continue to do so. To the administration, faculty, and staff at Annville-Cleona School District – your support means the world to me. To my little Yorkie, Gia – thank you for being the inspiration behind Poppy's adorable dog Pickle. To William Shakespeare – my greatest inspiration.

Finally, a special thank you to my husband. Even though you make fun of my "teeny-bopper" TV viewing habits and my ramblings about crazy middle-grade ideas, I could not successfully juggle a full-time teaching job and a writing career without the support of you and our amazing son, Bennett. So to both of you – thank you for holding down the fort while I have my "write time" during many evenings and weekends. I love you both to the moon!

JENNIE K. BROWN

Jennie K. Brown is an award-winning high school English teacher, freelance magazine writer, and author of children's books. She currently serves as president of the Pennsylvania Council of Teachers of English and Language Arts (PCTELA) and is an active member of SCBWI, NCTE, and ALAN. She is a regular contributor to the SCBWI Eastern PA and PCTELA blogs. When she's not teaching or writing, Jennie can be found reading, hanging out with her awesome family, or plotting her next book. Learn more about Jennie at jenniekbrown.com!

SAMPLE CHAPTERS

Poppy Mayberry,

Return to Power Academy

NOVA KIDS BOOK 2

Prologue

The first time I got in trouble for using my fantabulous mind-reading Thursday power was sitting in the middle of Mr. Salmon's 6th grade math class.

I almost missed the perfect mind reading opportunity because Mr. Salmon's giant toupee was bouncing on the top of his head as he walked across the front of the room and was totally distracting me. I chuckled, thinking of its resemblance to a furry, gray squirrel just hanging out on his head.

"Psst," I heard from behind me. I turned around and saw Mark Masters. His index finger was jammed up his nose – the bad habit he'd not been able to kick. His other hand pointed to the toupee king who now stood in front of me.

"Miss Mayberry," Mr. Salmon droned.

"Yes," I responded, polite as ever.

"Can you tell the class the square root of 49?"

Of course, I knew the answer was seven. When in doubt, I always answer seven. I just love that number.

Seven days in a week, after all.

"Seven," I said.

He grimaced and took a step closer to me. Did he really have to pick on me? He was a mind reading Thursday and totally read the toupee thought out of my head, and I was more sure than ever that was why he was attempting to call me out in the middle of class.

"Alright. That was an easy one," he said, pushing the thick wire-rimmed glasses up his nose. "Now tell everyone the square root of 657." A huge smirk formed on his face.

I thought back to our homework from last night, but nothing came to me. Sometimes I wished that my Monday power could miraculously conjure up answers, just as quickly as it allowed me to move things with my mind.

I glanced over at my former archenemy, Ellie Preston, and tried to read the answer from her head. She shook her head two times, meaning she had no idea what the answer was. Ellie had many strengths, but mathematics was definitely not one of them.

"That's what I thought, Miss Mayberry," Mr. Salmon said through a smile. The class giggled.

He turned his back from me and walked down the aisle. *That's what you get for making fun of my stylish hair.* I read that thought right of his mind.

"I wouldn't call it stylish," I spoke quietly, not knowing what compelled me to actually say it aloud when I could have just thought it right back at him. I hoped he hadn't heard me, but by the look in Mr. Salmon's eyes, he had most definitely heard the words that popped out of my mouth.

"Excuse me, Poppy?" Mr. Salmon said, walking back toward my seat. His hair bounced with each step and I chuckled to myself. At this point, all eyes were on me.

I responded meekly, "I just said, I wouldn't call your hair stylish." Giggles came from every direction. Did I seriously just make fun of my teacher in front of the class? This would so not be good.

"I need to speak with you in the hall, Miss Mayberry," Mr. Salmon stated, using his hand to slick the furry madness down while a slight pink color dabbled his cheeks. His tone was dead serious. The other Nova Middle students made all the typical "ohhhs" and "ahhhs" when anyone is sent out to the hall.

"I know exactly what you did in there," he said, nodding his head toward the classroom door, "and I know you're getting used to this new found Thursday-ness, but you know the rules about power usage in school!"

I could tell that Mr. Salmon was getting flustered, just like he did any time he had to yell at a student. He was so odd.

"It is one thing to read the thoughts from peoples' minds, but quite another for making those thoughts known!" he whisper-yelled, and his face began to turn an orangish-pink shade. "You don't want to spend another summer at Power Academy, do you?" he asked.

Of course I didn't want to go back there. But I couldn't stop staring at the color spreading across his face. "Mr. Salmon, you're turning salmon."

Mr. Salmon's hands shot up to his face. "I, umm, I," he stammered. "Just don't do it again," he said, whipping around quickly and slamming the classroom door behind. I just stood there, not knowing what to do next.

I smiled to myself, thanking my lucky stars I didn't get sent to Principal Wobble-Wible's office. That's when I, Poppy Rose Mayberry, knew that being a telekinetic Monday AND a telepathic Thursday could actually get me into trouble. But it could also be a lot of fun!

Chapter 1

Six Months Later

Now here I stood – at Power Academy yet again. I laughed to myself as I stepped under the giant arch at the entrance of the academy. Just like the welcome last year, greasy Mr. Grimeley was handing out one of those squishy stress ball thingies. It read the same thing – *Embrace Your Day. Be Special.* Totally weird. Couldn't they be a bit more creative this year?

Grimeley himself didn't change much. His pants were still in good need of seaming. The bottoms of his slacks curled under his unpolished shoes, and a swishing sound was heard as the fabric brushed against the ground with every step he took.

It had been exactly one year since I entered the Academy for the first time. One year since meeting crazy Clothes-too-tight Headmistress Larriby and her greasy sidekick Mr. Grimeley. One year since I made new friends in Logan, a disappearing Friday, and Sam, a light manipulating Wednesday. One year since my arch-nemesis, mind reading

Thursday Ellie Preston, became one of my all-time favorite people. And, exactly one year since the crazy summer adventure started when I found out for the first time that I was not only a telekinetic Monday, but also a mind reading Thursday. A "cusper," Mayor Masters had told me, and the rest of my friends. Even though I didn't know yet exactly what that meant.

But after all the drama of last summer – Pickle, my adorable and furry little Yorkie was hidden from me by crazy Larriby and greasy Grimeley – I definitely needed a little bit of convincing when Mayor Masters asked me to come back this summer as a newly appointed camp counselor. And Ellie was the one to do just that.

**

"Poppy – if you aren't going with me, I will like seriously die," Ellie had exaggerated, yet again, while plopping herself down on the giant purple papazan chair in the corner of my bedroom. Pickle had jumped up on her lap and was begging to have her ears rubbed.

I looked at Ellie and frowned, thinking of last summer's shenanigans and what an embarrassment I was at first with my lack of skills in the whole power department.

"Just think, Poppy. It's only six weeks this summer!" Ellie had smiled at me, her legs now curled under her on the oversized chair. She was right. I could do six weeks. On the bright side, it was much better than being there for an entire summer.

"And then we can be back to lounging by the pool, sipping on lemonade?" I asked, and she nodded her assurance.

So after a bit of deliberation, I decided, what the heck? A few weeks at Power Academy couldn't be that bad. Right? Plus, at least this time we were getting paid.

***

So here I was now, taking the ball from greasy Mr. Grimeley. I opened Pickle's crate, and threw it in – just like last year.

"Hey, Ellie!" I yelled, as we walked into Power Academy together.

Chapter 2

And so it began. Clothes-too-tight Headmistress Larriby wobbled her way down the center aisle of Power Academy's library. Today she looked like a rotting tomato. A giant rotting tomato to be exact. The red dress hugged her curves in all the wrong places, and spots of brown fluffy fabric dotted it. This was definitely not one of her best looks. Well ... she's never had a good look at all.

I glanced around to see about forty wannabe weekday students buzzing with anticipation. The Mondays were in a corner focusing, pointing fingers, squinting eyes, and attempting to make things move with their minds. To think, I was one of them last year.

A group of Wednesdays stared at the light fixture in the middle of the room. I read their minds, but they were totally empty, putting every ounce of energy into their lack of power. All those poor Wednesdays wanted to do was flip the lights on and off a few times, but by the constipated look on their faces, they were definitely struggling. Not even the slightest spark few from their fingertips.

"Psssst." I turned around to see Logan suddenly appear behind me. My cheeks grew warm. They did that every time he showed up. He was just too cute. He nodded his head in Larriby's direction. I didn't have to be a mind reading Thursday to know that he was thinking the same thing about her outfit as me.

"Where have you been?" I whispered. I glanced at the clock to note it was 9:15. An hour later than when we were supposed to report.

"You know, got caught up at home with Gram and Pops," he said, smiling that crooked smile at me. Not only was he a disappearing Friday, but Logan had the luxury of being one of the few teleporting Tuesdays at Power Academy. Sometimes I thought I wanted to be a teleporting Tuesday, but I prefer moving things and reading minds. Anyway, I was happy that Logan had two powers to focus on. I mean, I kind of felt sorry for him. Both of his parents passed away years ago and he has to live with his powerless grandparents.

A piece of dirty blond bang fell into Logan's eye. With a simple flick of my wrist, I willed the hair to shoot straight back his head. I chuckled at the Mr. Greasy Grimeley-esque comb over I just gave him.

"Thanks a lot, Poppy," he said through a smirk. His hand ruffled the hairs back into their original position. I remembered back to last summer when I could barely even move a feather with my mind. Now I'd practically perfected my power. Gone are the days of flying spaghetti sticking to my dad's bald head, Pickle getting hit by out of control dog brushes, and headbands violently shattering against chalkboards. Now when there's a disaster and I use my powers, I do it on purpose.

"So has anyone talked to you about what we're actually doing here?"

"Nope, not at all," I said, pulling my out-of-control curly red hair into a messy bun – something Ellie Preston had recently helped me perfect. Seriously, my hair was a disaster zone last year. "Mayor Masters said that we'd be helping the powerless and stuff, but she never mentioned the specifics," I said, looking over his shoulder at Clothes-too-tight Larriby and Mayor Masters (nose-picking Mark's mom and the Mayor of Nova) in a heated discussion.

"Well, if it's anything like last year, I'm out," he said, leaning back in his chair, arms crossed over his chest.

His comment brought me back to those few awful weeks at the prison that was Power Academy. In order to help us come into our weekday powers last summer, Larriby and Grimeley had hidden our personal items from us. My precious dog Pickle had been locked up in a cage in the middle of a supposedly haunted forest. In the end, I guess we did master our powers, and learned that we were *cuspers*. I still hadn't completely warmed up to Clothes-too-tight

Larriby and her greasy sidekick Grimeley though.

"Who's that?" Logan asked, taking me from my thoughts. Waltzing down the middle of the library aisle was a man that had the letters N.P.C. stitched into the upper right pocket of his jacket. A wide brimmed black hat was pulled down low over his eyes. He was not your typical-looking Power Academy instructor, especially with those tight black skinny jeans (yuck), but for some reason he looked familiar to me. As he lifted his head to talk to Headmistress Larriby, I realized exactly where I'd seen him before. I thought back to last week at Novalicious, when I'd told my other best friend, Veronica White, about my plans for the start of summer. She had been more than bummed.

***

"So, you're telling me that you're going to spend every single day the next two months at Power Academy?" Veronica blinked hard. "With Ellie?"

Veronica and I had been best friends since … well … forever, and she was still getting used to the fact that my ex-enemy Ellie Preston and I were now seeing eye to eye. I wanted to be completely honest with Veronica about the whole cusp power thing, but we had all promised Mayor

Masters that we would keep that to ourselves. That was something else Ellie and I had in common that I didn't have with Veronica. Even though Veronica had no clue about the whole mind reading thing, she had definitely sensed a stronger connection between Ellie and me over the last year. I guess I couldn't blame her for being a little jealous.

"It's actually only six weeks," I said as I threw the Power Academy brochure down on the table in front of her. The bright greens and blues on the pamphlet made the place look pretty appealing. I was happy to see they'd revamped the brochure from last year.

Using her Monday power, she pushed the pamphlet back to my side of that table and took a lick of her cone, totally avoiding eye contact.

Did she have to be so dramatic?

During the gap of awkward silence, I had glanced around Novalicious to see all sorts of other people using their weekday powers. Niel Porter, a boy that was in my 5th period history class used his telekinesis power to suspend three cones in mid-air as he reached for a fourth. After paying at the counter, Mr. Ellison and his son Trevor (both Tuesdays who frequented Novalicious) vanished into thin air. Obviously they teleported back home.

I glanced back at Veronica just in time to see her smiling at me. She was back to her normal non-jealous self. "Look, Poppy. You are totally going to be fantabulous helping those other students," Ronni stated in between bites of her two scoops of peanut-butter, chocolate chip goodness. "I'm sorry I get a bit—" She stopped mid-sentence. Her eyes widened at the sight of whoever just walked through the glass door. "Look! Look! It's one of *them*," she said, wiping her face with the back of her hand. Her head nodded toward the entrance of Novalicious.

I turned around to see a tall, skinny man in a long black jacket shuffling through the line. On the upper right corner of his coat was a shield emblem containing the initials N.P.C.. His black baseball-style cap had the same exact lettering.

"Those Nova Power Corp. guys totally freak me out," I whispered, leaning forward in my chair and away from him as he passed behind me.

"What about your dad?" Ronni asked. "Does he freak you out too?"

"Very funny." I said, unenthusiastically. My dad does work at Nova Power Corporation, but he's a security guard, not whatever this guy was. I stole a glance over my shoulder. The man's dark eyes scanned across Novalicious from one person to the next. I'd seen that look enough times to know that he was a mind reading Thursday. When his eyes met mine, they lingered on me for just long enough to make a shiver run down my spine. My default thought of dog poop entered my head.

"He's obviously looking for something," Veronica said, leaning in closer to me.

I swallowed. "Or someone. Dun. Dun. Dun," I added ominously.

The man got in line behind Mr. and Mrs. Ream – two poor, powerless weekends.

"Or maybe he's come to personally escort you to Power Academy," Veronica said with a giggle, lightening the mood even more. I was glad to have my BFF back, and not the jealous person who sat across from me just a few minutes ago.

"Yeah, right!" Over the last year, under the direction of Mayor Masters, Nova Power Corp. moved its location to the grounds of Power Academy due to some space issues, so it wasn't entirely out of the question considering the logo on his jacket. Nevertheless, it was still laughable that he would venture outside of N.P.C. to pick up a measly Monday (and semi-Thursday) who was still getting used to her new mind reading power.

"What a weirdo!" she said as we watched his head move mechanically from side to side, scoping out the scene. Suddenly, the little ol' creepster whipped his head around toward us. This time his eyes lingered on me even longer than they did earlier.

"Oh. Em. Gee … do you think he heard us?" Veronica said.

"Nah. Just a coincidence," I said, but I wasn't entirely sure. Ever since he entered Novalicious, I had the strange feeling that he wasn't focusing on anyone but me.

Veronica pulled the hair tie from her ponytail and let a few black strands fall in front of her face. "Okay, for serious though. Now he is totally starting to creep me out," she whispered.

"Is he still looking in this direction?" I asked. The creepy man had moved up in line, so now my back was to him.

Veronica's eyes slowly moved from my forehead and then up a bit farther. "Yep," Veronica said without moving her lips. I really wanted to tell her about my new power. She nodded.

"Let's finish up here," I said. Veronica and I licked our ice cream as fast as we could. My head started pounding from brain freeze.

I stood up and could now see the man sitting at a table near the only door in Novalicious. He just sat there with a glass of water. The creeper didn't even order a drink, let alone a cone, so there was no reason for him to be skulking around.

"Are you almost done?" I asked Veronica, grabbing the orange pendant suspended from my neck. My purple ballet flat tapped on the floor below. I wanted to get the heck out of there. With a quick twist at her hand, Veronica's trash lifted from her hand, gently flew across the room, and landed in the trashcan directly to the creepy guy's right.

We rushed out of Novalicious as fast as our legs could carry us, but with each step, I could feel the man's eyes on me.

And then, it got even stranger. As we left, Mayor Masters flew past us without a glance or even a hello, which was so unlike her.

"That's weird," I said. Her son, nose picking Mark Masters, has been in like all of our classes the last five years. That and the personal invitation to be a Power Academy counselor made it even odder that she walked by without saying a word.

"Rude, much? And how long have we been friends with Mark?" Veronica said with an eye roll.

I thought of the many times Veronica had not-so-subtly called Mark out on his, ahem, nose-picking habit.

"I didn't realize you'd consider him a friend?" I said, not meaning for it to come out as harsh as it did. Thinking back now, I probably should have kept my mouth shut.

"And what's that supposed to mean?" she snarked, stopping dead in her tracks.

"Nothing. Just forget about it," I said, hoping she would. Ever since Ellie started hanging out with us, Veronica had been even more touchy than usual.

"I have to go," she spat, turning to walk in the opposite direction. "Say hi to you BFF Ellie for me." Her black combat-style boots stomped away.

Before I even had the chance to yell after her, Ronni had turned the corner and made her way out of sight. That was not the way I wanted to leave my best friend before six weeks away at Power Academy.

***

And now, that same creeper guy that Veronica and I saw at Novalicious was here. At Power Academy. I glanced at Clothes-too-tight Larriby just in time to see a scowl form on her face. Whoever this man was, she was not happy to see him. The mysterious man walked straight up to the stage and leaned in close to Larriby. Her face contorted into an even bigger frown as he whispered in her ear.

"Come on," Logan said, glancing in my direction. "Use your Thursday skills, Poppy. Larriby looks mad."

I concentrated really hard on Headmistress Larriby. I wanted to see what she was thinking of this guy's comments. Typically, when I did this, I was greeted with a few words flying through my head here and there. It was easy to get the gist of somebody's thoughts. But right now I got nothing but static.

"Well?"

"Nothing," I said with a frown. "Too many other weekday thoughts flying around. It's distracting."

The strange man drew back from Larriby and then proceeded to walk back up the aisle in our direction. As he reached the row where I was seated, his eyes caught mine just like they did at Novalicious.

"I wish he'd just go away," I whispered to Logan.

By the scowl on Headmistress Larriby's face, she didn't want him here either.

OTHER MONTH9BOOKS TITLES YOU MIGHT LIKE

POLARIS

ARTIFACTS

HAIR IN ALL THE WRONG PLACES

Find more awesome Teen books at http://www. Month9Books.com

Connect with Month9Books online:

Facebook: www.Facebook.com/Month9Books

Twitter: https://twitter.com/Month9Books

You Tube: www.youtube.com/user/Month9Books

Blog: www.month9booksblog.com

Request review copies via publicity@month9books.com

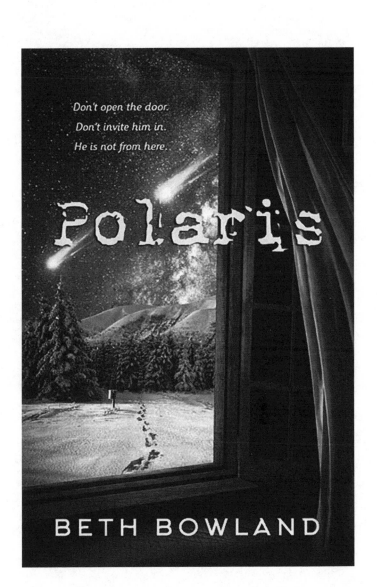

Don't open the door.

Don't invite him in.

He is not from here.

Polaris

BETH BOWLAND

ANDREW BUCKLEY
HAIR IN ALL THE WRONG PLACES
WHAT'S HAPPENING TO HIM? WHAT HAS HE DONE?
AND WHAT ON EARTH IS THAT SMELL?